THE NATIVE STORIES FROM KEEPERS OF THE EARTH

Told by JOSEPH BRUCHAC

Michael J. Caduto and Joseph Bruchac

Illustrations by John Kahionhes Fadden

FIFTH HOUSE PUBLISHERS
SASKATOON, SASKATCHEWAN

First Canadian Edition

Cover Illustration by John Kahionhes Fadden

Cover Design and Colorization by Hugh Anderson, Archetype, Inc.
Interior Design by Karen Groves, Fulcrum Publishing

Canadian Cataloging-in-Publication Data
Bruchac, Joseph, 1942–
The Native Stories from Keepers of the Earth
Canadian ed. –
ISBN 0-920079-76-8
1. Indians of North America - Legends
2. Indians of North America - Religion and mythology - Juvenile literature
I. Caduto, Michael J. Keepers of the Earth
II. Title
E98.F6B78 1991 j398.2/089/97 C91-097066-1

Printed and bound in the United States of America
2 3 4 93 92 91

Fifth House Publishers
620 Duchess Street
Saskatoon, SK,
S7K 0R1

The poem "Birdfoot's Grampa" by Joseph Bruchac is from Joseph Bruchac's *Entering Onondaga* (1978) published by Cold Mountain Press and reprinted here with the permission of the author.

The map on pages *xiv–xv* showing the culture regions of Native American groups discussed in this book, is printed with permission of Michael J. Caduto (© 1989). Cartography by Stacy Miller, Upper Marlboro, Maryland.

The cover illustration and the story illustrations throughout this book by John Kahionhes Fadden are reprinted with his permission.

For the children of yesterday, today and tomorrow

Birdfoot's Grampa

The old man
must have stopped our car
two dozen times to climb out
and gather into his hands
the small toads blinded
by our lights and leaping,
live drops of rain.

The rain was falling,
a mist about his white hair
and I kept saying
you can't save them all,
accept it, get back in
we've got places to go.

But, leathery hands full
of wet brown life,
knee deep in the summer
roadside grass,
he just smiled and said
they have places to go to
too.

—Joseph Bruchac
Entering Onondaga

Contents

Foreword by N. Scott Momaday *vii*
Introduction *ix*
Map Showing the Cultural Areas and Tribal Locations of Native North American Groups *xii*

Creation
The Coming of Gluscabi
Abenaki—Northeast Woodlands 3
The Earth on Turtle's Back
Onondaga—Northeast Woodlands 5
Four Worlds: The Dine Story of Creation
Dine [Navajo]—Southwest 11

Fire
Loo-Wit, the Fire-Keeper
Nisqually—Pacific Northwest 21
How Grandmother Spider Stole the Sun
Muskogee [Creek]—Oklahoma 27

Earth
Tunka-shila, Grandfather Rock
Lakota [Sioux]—Great Plains 33
Old Man Coyote and the Rock
Pawnee—Great Plains 35

Wind and Weather
Gluscabi and the Wind Eagle
Abenaki—Northeast Woodlands 41

Water
The Hero Twins and the Swallower of Clouds
Zuni—Southwest 53

Koluscap and the Water Monster
Micmac and Maliseet—Maritime Provinces 59
How Thunder and Earthquake Made Ocean
Yurok—California 63
Sedna, the Woman Under the Sea
Inuit—Arctic Regions 67
How Raven Made the Tides
Tsimshian—Pacific Northwest 73

Sky
How Coyote Was the Moon
Kalispel—Idaho 77
How Fisher Went to the Skyland: The Origin of the Big Dipper
Anishinabe—Great Lakes Region 79

Seasons
Spring Defeats Winter
Seneca—Northeast Woodlands 89

Plants and Animals
The Coming of Corn
Cherokee—North Carolina 95
Manabozho and the Maple Trees
Anishinabe—Great Lakes Region 99
Kokopilau, the Hump-Backed Flute Player
Hopi—Southwest 101
How Turtle Flew South for the Winter
Dakota [Sioux]—Midwest 105
Gluscabi and the Game Animals
Abenaki—Northeast Woodlands 109
Awi Usdi, the Little Deer
Cherokee—North Carolina 115

Life, Death, Spirit
The Origin of Death
Siksika [Blackfeet]—Montana and Alberta 121

Unity of Earth
The White Buffalo Calf Woman and the Sacred Pipe
Lakota [Sioux]—Great Plains 127

Glossary and Pronunciation Key 131
Tribal Nation Descriptions 139

Foreword

"Who are you?" someone asks.

"I am the story of myself," comes the answer.

It is true that man invests himself in story. And it is true, as someone has said, that God made man because He loves stories.

In his traditional world the Native American lives in the presence of stories. The storyteller is one whose spirit is indispensable to the people. He is magician, artist and creator. And, above all, he is a holy man. His is a sacred business.

How are we to come to an understanding of the storyteller and his art? It will be useful, perhaps, to consider the following tenets.

Stories are made of words and of such implications as the storyteller places upon words. The story lies at the center of language, and language is composed of words. Words, then, are the primary tools of the storyteller. It is to his purpose to use words well.

There are many kinds of stories. The basic story is one which centers upon an event, and the words proceed toward the formulation of meaning. This is the narrative process. The storyteller sets words in procession; his object is most often the establishment of meaning.

In general, stories are true to human experience. Indeed, the truth of human experience is their principal information. This is to say that stories tend to support and confirm our perceptions of the world and of the creatures within it. Even the most fantastic story is rooted in our common experience; otherwise, it would have no meaning for us. Strictly speaking, it would not be a story.

Stories are formed. The formation of the story is particular and perceptible. The storyteller proceeds according to a plan, a design, a sense of proportion and order. Stories are begun, they proceed and they come to an end.

Stories are predicated upon belief. Belief is more essential to the story than is understanding.

The storyteller creates his listener. In effect the storyteller says to his listener, "In my story I determine you; for a moment—the duration of the story—your reason for being is the story itself; for the sake of the story, you are. In my story I create a state of being in which you are immediately involved."

The primary object of the story is the realization of wonder and delight.

For nearly twenty years I have taught the subject of Native American oral tradition, and I have been a student of that subject for a longer time than that. I have found these several tenets especially relevant to the whole matter of storytelling. The stories in the present collection center upon one of the most important of all considerations in human experience: the relationship between man and nature. In the Native American world this relationship is so crucial as to be definitive of the way in which man formulates his own best idea of himself. In the presence of these stories we have an affirmation of the human spirit. It is a just and wondrous celebration.

—N. Scott Momaday

Introduction

The Earth is our Mother
The Sun is our Father
—*Okanagan saying*

The native people of North America speak of their relationship to the Earth in terms of family. The Earth is not something to be bought and sold, something to be used and mistreated. It is, quite simply, the source of our lives—our Mother. And the rest of Creation, all around us, shares in that family relationship. The Okanagan people of the Pacific Northwest speak of the Earth as Mother, the Sun as Father and the animals as our brothers and sisters. This view of the world was held by the Navajo and the Abenaki, the Sioux and the Anishinabe and most of the aboriginal people of this continent. They saw their role on this Earth, not as rulers of Creation, but as beings entrusted with a very special mission—to maintain the natural balance, to take care of our Mother, to be Keepers of the Earth. Life was seen as a great circle; each person had a place on that circle and was related to everyone and everything. Even an individual life could be seen as a circle, beginning with Creation and ending, not with death, but with a return to Creation itself. The very old and the very young were close to each other on that circle, because the beginning and the end of a life were near each other on that round, just as winter is close to spring.

Of course, being human, not every native person remembered this all the time. Just like the people of European descent who came later to North America, the aboriginal people sometimes forgot the role they were supposed to play in the natural world and forgot to respect their elders or to share with others. However, the native people had the benefit of thousands of years of living *with*, not just *on*, this place they called Turtle Island, this land balanced on the back of a great Turtle. As a result, they developed ways of living and ways of teaching that enabled them to blend into the land, to sustain not just themselves, but generations to come. It is commonly said among the native people of the Northeast, for example, that we must always consider the results of our deeds on the seventh generation after our own. The knowledge that native people obtained from thousands of years of living and seeking balance, was, in a very real sense, quite scientific. But it was not taught to their people in classrooms or in books; instead, it was taught in two very powerful ways. The first way was through experience, the second through oral tradition, especially through the telling of stories.

The stories in this collection, which come from *Keepers of the Earth*—a book that unites western scientific methods and Native American traditional stories—can be called "lesson stories." All come from native oral traditions. They have been chosen because the lessons they teach are relatively easy for nonnative people to understand. Some of these stories have more than one lesson to teach. As Joseph Campbell explains in *The Power of Myth*, the same stories mean different things to us at different times in our lives, and as we grow, those stories grow with us. The story of Gluscabi and the game animals is one such story. While using this story in workshops, my coauthor Michael Caduto and I have asked people how many lessons are taught by this one tale. No group ever comes up with fewer than a dozen.

The traditional use of these stories was always twofold. First, of course, the stories were meant to entertain. Second, and more important, they were meant to teach. If a child misbehaved, that child would not be struck or humiliated; instead, a lesson story would be told. Striking a child breaks that child's spirit, serves as a bad example and seldom teaches the right lesson. But a story goes into a person and remains there. And children aren't the only ones who can be taught by the use of lesson stories.

For storytellers, parents and teachers who wish to use these stories here are some suggestions. First, it is important to know a story well before telling it. Read a story many times before attempting to tell it to someone else. Second, knowing a people's stories also means knowing a people. A good approach to each of these tales is to find out as much as possible about the *specific* tribal nation the story comes from. Start with the glossary and the tribal nation descriptions at the end of this book, but don't stop there. Continue not only through books, but also through meeting contemporary Native American people. A helpful new book is the travel guide *Indian America* (John Muir Publications, 1990) by Eagle Walking Turtle. Good places to meet Native Americans are pow wows, yearly festivals that take place in summer and fall all over North America, where native people sell food and crafts, dress in traditional costumes, dance and sing.

Third, these stories are meant to be told aloud. They become more alive when they are spoken. As you are telling the stories, pause every now and then and say the word "Ho?" Tell your listeners to respond with "Hey!" each time they hear you say "Ho?" By involving your listeners in the story, you enable them to feel more a part of the story. Remember when you tell stories to speak slowly and clearly; don't rush your stories.

Fourth and most important, remember to listen. There are stories all around you. No matter who you are, you have a tradition of storytelling as your heritage. It may not be Native American; it may be Irish or Latvian,

Japanese or Ashanti, but it is there. Look to the stories of your own birthright, and try to understand the lessons they teach you about your own life and the world around you. This book should be only a beginning for your travel on the circle of stories. Like all circles, it has no end.

—Joseph Bruchac (Sozap)
Penibagos Kisos/Long Nights Moon 1990

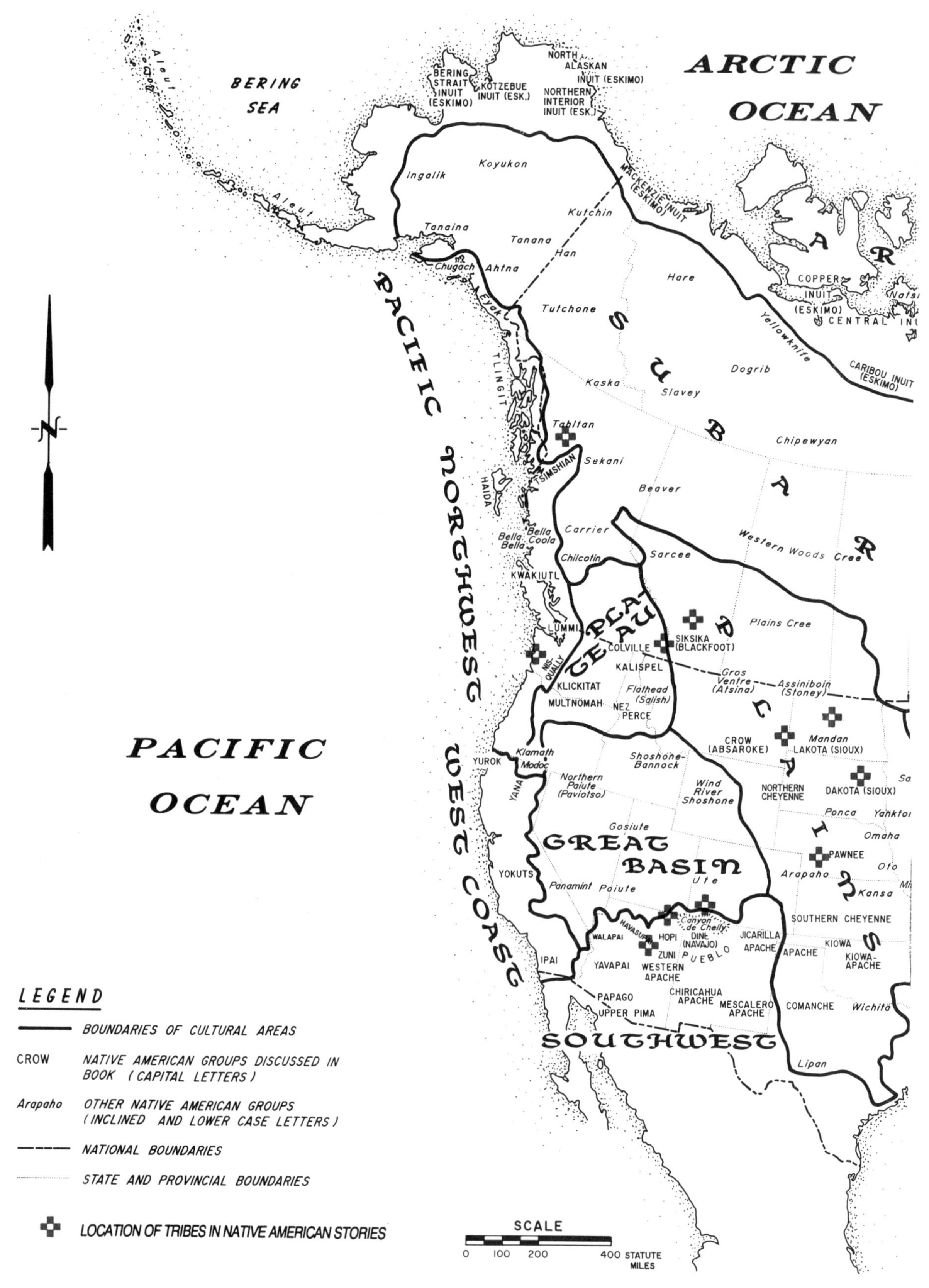

ARCTIC OCEAN
BERING SEA
PACIFIC OCEAN
Aleut
BERING STRAIT INUIT (ESKIMO)
KOTZEBUE INUIT (ESK.)
NORTH ALASKAN INUIT (ESKIMO)
NORTHERN INTERIOR INUIT (ESK.)
MACKENZIE INUIT (ESKIMO)
Ingalik
Koyukon
Kutchin
Tanaina
Tanana
Han
Chugach
Ahtna
Eyak
Tutchone
Hare
COPPER INUIT (ESKIMO)
CENTRAL INU
Yellowknife
Dogrib
CARIBOU INUIT (ESKIMO)
TLINGIT
Kaska
Slavey
Tahltan
Sekani
Chipewyan
TSIMSHIAN
HAIDA
Beaver
Bella Bella
Bella Coola
Carrier
Chilcotin
Sarcee
Western Woods Cree
KWAKIUTL
LUMMI
NISQUALLY
SIKSIKA (BLACKFOOT)
Plains Cree
COLVILLE
KALISPEL
Gros Ventre (Atsina)
Assiniboin (Stoney)
KLICKITAT
Flathead (Salish)
MULTNOMAH
NEZ PERCE
CROW (ABSAROKE)
Mandan
LAKOTA (SIOUX)
Klamath
Modoc
YUROK
Shoshone-Bannock
Northern Paiute (Paviotso)
YANA
Wind River Shoshone
NORTHERN CHEYENNE
DAKOTA (SIOUX)
Ponca
Yankton
Gosiute
Omaha
PAWNEE
Oto
YOKUTS
Arapaho
Ute
Panamint
Paiute
Kansa
SOUTHERN CHEYENNE
Canyon de Chelly
WALAPAI
HAVASUPAI
HOPI
DINE (NAVAJO)
JICARILLA APACHE
APACHE
KIOWA
KIOWA-APACHE
ZUNI
PUEBLO
IPAI
YAVAPAI
WESTERN APACHE
PAPAGO
CHIRICAHUA APACHE
MESCALERO APACHE
COMANCHE
Wichita
UPPER PIMA
Lipan
PACIFIC NORTHWEST COAST
SUBARCTIC
PLATEAU
PLAINS
GREAT BASIN
SOUTHWEST
N
LEGEND
BOUNDARIES OF CULTURAL AREAS
CROW
NATIVE AMERICAN GROUPS DISCUSSED IN BOOK (CAPITAL LETTERS)
Arapaho
OTHER NATIVE AMERICAN GROUPS (INCLINED AND LOWER CASE LETTERS)
NATIONAL BOUNDARIES
STATE AND PROVINCIAL BOUNDARIES
LOCATION OF TRIBES IN NATIVE AMERICAN STORIES
SCALE
0 100 200 400 STATUTE MILES

Cultural areas and tribal locations of Native North Americans. This map shows tribal locations as they appeared around 1600, except for the Seminole Indians in the southeast and the Tuscaroras in the northeast. The Seminoles formed from a group which withdrew from the Muskogee (Creek) Indians and joined with several other groups on the Georgia/Florida border to form the Seminoles, a name which has been used since about 1775. In the eastern woodlands the Haudenausaunee (Iroquois) consist of six nations, the Mohawk, Oneida, Onondaga, Cayuga, Seneca and Tuscarora. The Tuscaroras were admitted to the Iroquois League in 1722 after many refugees from the Tuscarora Wars (1711–1713) in the southeast fled northward. The Wabanaki Peoples include the Micmac, Maliseet, Passamaquoddy, Abenaki, Penobscot and Pennacook.

NATIVE NORTH AMERICA

Creation

"I am wonderful because you sprinkled me."

Abenaki

Northeast Woodlands

The Coming of Gluscabi

After Tabaldak had finished making human beings, he dusted his hands off and some of that dust sprinkled on the Earth.

From that dust Gluscabi formed himself. He sat up from the Earth and said, "Here I am." So it is that some of the Abenaki people call Gluscabi by another name, "Odzihozo," which means, "the man who made himself from something." He was not as powerful as Tabaldak, The Owner, but like his grandchildren, the human beings, he had the power to change things, sometimes for the worse.

When Gluscabi sat up from the Earth, The Owner was astonished. "How did it happen now that you came to be?" he said.

Then Gluscabi said, "Well, it is because I formed myself from this dust left over from the first humans that you made."

"You are very wonderful," The Owner told him.

"I am wonderful because you sprinkled me," Gluscabi answered.

"Let us roam around now," said The Owner. So they left that place and went uphill to the top of a mountain. There they gazed about, open-eyed, so far around they could see. They could see the lakes, the rivers, the trees, how all the land lay, the Earth.

Then The Owner said, "Behold here how wonderful is my work. By the wish of my mind I created all this existing world, oceans, rivers, lakes." And he and Gluscabi gazed open-eyed.

They could see the lakes, the rivers, the trees, how all the land lay, the Earth.

Onondaga

Northeast Woodlands

The Earth on Turtle's Back

Before this Earth existed, there was only water.

It stretched as far as one could see, and in that water there were birds and animals swimming around. Far above, in the clouds, there was a Skyland. In that Skyland there was a great and beautiful tree. It had four white roots which stretched to each of the sacred directions, and from its branches all kinds of fruits and flowers grew.

There was an ancient chief in the Skyland. His young wife was expecting a child, and one night she dreamed that she saw the Great Tree uprooted. The next morning she told her husband the story.

He nodded as she finished telling her dream. "My wife," he said, "I am sad that you had this dream. It is clearly a dream of great power and, as is our way, when one has such a powerful dream we must do all

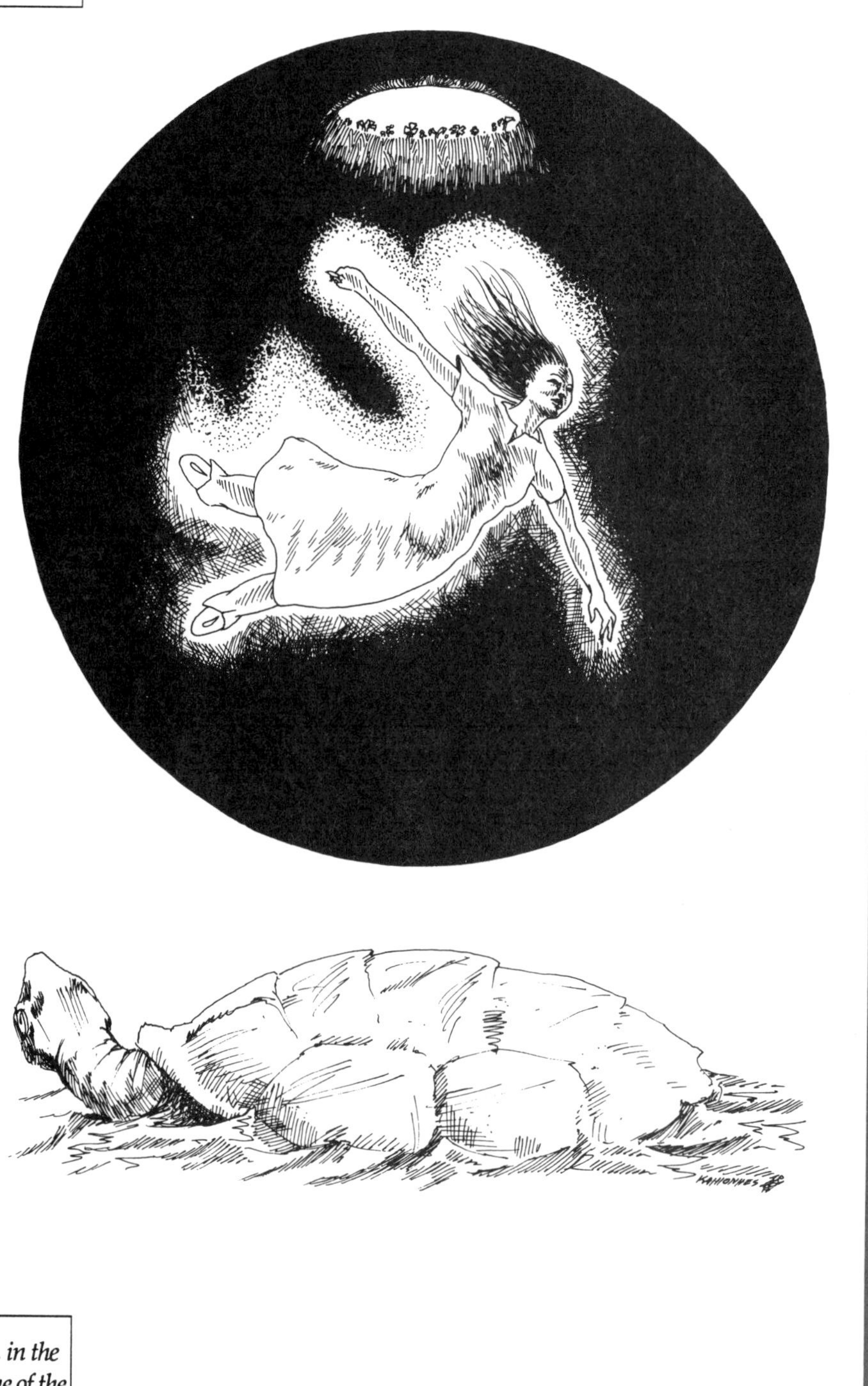

Far below, in the waters, some of the birds and animals looked up.

that we can to make it true. The Great Tree must be uprooted."

Then the ancient chief called the young men together and told them that they must pull up the tree. But the roots of the tree were so deep, so strong, that they could not budge it. At last the ancient chief himself came to the tree. He wrapped his arms around it, bent his knees and strained. At last, with one great effort, he uprooted the tree and placed it on its side. Where the tree's roots had gone deep into the Skyland there was now a big hole. The wife of the chief came close and leaned over to look down, grasping the tip of one of the Great Tree's branches to steady her. It seemed as if she saw something down there, far below, glittering like water. She leaned out further to look and, as she leaned, she lost her balance and fell into the hole. Her hand slipped off the tip of the branch, leaving her with only a handful of seeds as she fell, down, down, down, down.

Far below, in the waters, some of the birds and animals looked up.

"Someone is falling toward us from the sky," said one of the birds.

"We must do something to help her," said another. Then two Swans flew up. They caught the Woman From The Sky between their wide wings. Slowly, they began to bring

her down toward the water, where the birds and animals were watching.

"She is not like us," said one of the animals. "Look, she doesn't have webbed feet. I don't think she can live in the water."

"What shall we do, then?" said another of the water animals.

"I know," said one of the water birds. "I have heard that there is Earth far below the waters. If we dive down and bring up Earth, then she will have a place to stand."

So the birds and animals decided that someone would have to bring up Earth. One by one they tried.

The Duck dove down first, some say. He swam down and down, far beneath the surface, but could not reach the bottom and floated back up. Then the Beaver tried. He went even deeper, so deep that it was all dark, but he could not reach the bottom, either. The Loon tried, swimming with his strong wings. He was gone a long, long time, but he, too, failed to bring up Earth. Soon it seemed that all had tried and all had failed. Then a small voice spoke. "I will bring up Earth or die trying."

They looked to see who it was. It was the tiny Muskrat. She dove down and swam and swam. She was not as strong or as swift as the others, but she was determined.

They caught the Woman From The Sky between their wide wings.

She went so deep that it was all dark, and still she swam deeper. She went so deep that her lungs felt ready to burst, but she swam deeper still. At last, just as she was becoming unconscious, she reached out one small paw and grasped at the bottom, barely touching it before she floated up, almost dead.

When the other animals saw her break the surface they thought she had failed. Then they saw her right paw was held tightly shut.

"She has the Earth," they said. "Now where can we put it?"

"Place it on my back," said a deep voice. It was the Great Turtle, who had come up from the depths.

They brought the Muskrat over to the Great Turtle and placed her paw against his back. To this day there are marks at the back of the Turtle's shell which were made by Muskrat's paw. The tiny bit of Earth fell on the back of the Turtle. Almost immediately, it began to grow larger and larger and larger until it became the whole world.

Then the two Swans brought the Sky Woman down. She stepped onto the new Earth and opened her hand, letting the seeds fall onto the bare soil. From those seeds the trees and the grass sprang up. Life on Earth had begun.

The Big Reed grew up and up.

Four Worlds: The Dine Story of Creation

Before this world existed, there was a First World far below the world where we are now.

In that world everything was black. There was darkness everywhere, and in that darkness there were six beings. Those beings were First Man, the son of Night and the Blue Sky over the sunset; First Woman, the daughter of Day Break and the Yellow Sky of sunset; Salt Woman; Fire God; Coyote and Begochiddy. Begochiddy, who was the child of the Sun, was both man and woman, and had blue eyes and golden hair.

There were no mountains or plants in that first world, so Begochiddy began to make them. Begochiddy made four mountains. To the east Begochiddy made a white mountain. To the south Begochiddy made a blue mountain. To the west Begochiddy made a yellow mountain. To the north Begochiddy made a black mountain. Then Begochiddy created the ants and other insects and made the

first plants. But things were not right in that First World. One story is that Fire God became jealous and started to burn everything up. According to another story, the First Beings were just not happy in that dark world. Whatever the reason was, they decided to leave the First World.

"Gather together the plants and the other things I have made," said Begochiddy to First Man.

First Man did as Begochiddy said. Then he and the other beings came to the red mountain which Begochiddy created in the center of the First World. There Begochiddy planted the Big Reed. As the hollow Big Reed began to grow, the First Beings climbed into it. Up and up it grew, leaving the First World behind. It grew up and up until it came to the Second World.

In the Second World Begochiddy created even more things. Begochiddy created the clouds. Begochiddy created more plants and mountains. The color of the Second World was blue, and there were other beings in it—Swallow People and Cat People. The Cat People tried to fight Begochiddy and the others, but First Man used his magic and overcame them. For a time, everyone was happy. Then things began to go wrong. Once more Begochiddy planted Big Reed. Once more Begochiddy told First Man and the others to put all the things created into Big Reed. Big Reed began to grow. Up and up it went and carried them all to the Third World.

Whatever the reason was, they decided to leave the First World.

The Third World was yellow. Though there was no sun and no moon, the mountains gave light. It was the most beautiful of the worlds they had seen. In this world Begochiddy created rivers and springs. Begochiddy made water animals and trees, birds and lightning. Then Begochiddy created all kinds of human beings. In this beautiful Third World everything spoke one language. All of the things and beings in creation understood each other. But everything was not perfect in the Third World. Yellow and red streaks appeared across the eastern sky. They were placed there by First Man and represented the diseases about to come to the people through evil magic. Before long, the men and women began to quarrel with each other. The men said that the women were causing trouble. The women said that it was the men. Coyote came to Begochiddy and told him that men and women were always quarreling. Begochiddy decided to put a stop to it.

"All of the men," Begochiddy said, "must stay on the right bank of the river. All of the women must stay on the left bank. Neither may cross the river to be with the other."

So it was done. The men and women lived apart for some time, but they were not happy without each other. Finally they went to Begochiddy. Some say it was the women who came first, but others say it was the men.

"We are not happy by ourselves," they said. "We wish to be reunited."

So Begochiddy brought men and women back together.

"If there is more trouble," he warned them, "this Third World will be destroyed by a flood."

All of this time, Coyote was roaming around. Wherever he went he was curious about everything, including things he should have left well enough alone. One day, Salt Woman went walking by the two big rivers Begochiddy had made in this Third World. When she came to the place where the rivers crossed, she saw something strange in the water. It looked like a baby with long black hair. She went back and told the others about it. Coyote decided to go and see for himself. Sure enough, there where the rivers crossed was a baby with long black hair in the water. Coyote lifted it out of the water and hid it under his blanket. He told no one what he had done.

Four days passed and then a great noise was heard all around the Third World. Begochiddy knew what it was, knew what was going to happen. Someone had done wrong. Now this Third World was about to be destroyed by flood. From the east a black storm came. From the south a blue storm approached. From the west came a yellow storm. From the north a white storm swept. Once again Begochiddy gathered all the beings and things created. Once again Big Reed grew up and up. It lifted up all the beings and things as storm waters rose beneath them.

This time, though, was not as easy as before. Big Reed

Yellow and red streaks appeared across the eastern sky.

stopped growing before it entered the next world. The Spider People wove a web to bring them closer, but they could not break through into the new world. The Ant People tried to dig through, but they could not do it. Finally Begochiddy told the Locust to try. Using his hard head, the Locust broke through into the Fourth World. Now Begochiddy climbed up through the hole the Locust made. He found himself on an island with only water to be seen in all directions. Begochiddy saw right away that there were others in this Fourth World who had great power. To the east was Talking God. To the south was First Bringer of Seeds. To the west was House God. To the north was Second Bringer of Seeds. Begochiddy waved to each of them. Then the four powerful beings made the waters recede, leaving a world covered with mud. Begochiddy went back down Big Reed to the others.

"Grandparent," said the others, "how is it in the new world?"

"The new world is good," Begochiddy said, "but it has not yet dried. Someone must try to walk up there. Who will try?"

"I will go," said Badger. Then he went up through the hole and tried to walk on the new Fourth World. His feet broke through the surface, though, and became covered with mud. To this day all badgers have black feet.

"This will not do," Begochiddy said. "How can we dry this new world?"

All of this time, Coyote was roaming around.

"We shall dry it," said the winds. Then the winds went up to the Fourth World. The cyclones and the whirlwinds and the small dust devils went up to the Fourth World. They swirled about and dried the surface well so the people could walk. Then the Ant People went up and walked on the dried surface of the Fourth World, and all the other people and created things followed.

Begochiddy, though, looked back down through the hole to the Third World. The water there was still rising.

"Who is the one who angered the Water Monster?" Begochiddy said.

No one answered, but Coyote pulled his blanket tighter around himself.

"Open your blanket," Begochiddy said.

Then Coyote opened his blanket and Begochiddy saw the water baby.

"You must give the Water Monster back its child," said Begochiddy.

Coyote did as Begochiddy said. He dropped the water baby back down to the Third World, and the waters receded.

Now Begochiddy went around the Fourth World and

placed things in order. The mountains were put in their places. The Sun and Moon and Stars were put into the sky. Fire God tried to keep all the fire to himself, even though the people needed it to keep warm and cook their food. One night, though, as Fire God slept, Coyote stole fire from him and gave it to all the people. Then Begochiddy told the human beings the right way to live, how to give thanks, how to care for the plants such as corn and squash and beans. Begochiddy gave them many different languages, then, and sent them to live throughout the world. It was now, in this Fourth World, that Changing Woman came to be. She became the greatest friend of the human beings, helping them in many ways. It was Changing Woman who gave birth to the Hero Twins, who traveled throughout the world doing great deeds, destroying the monsters that threatened the people.

So the Fourth World came to be. However, just as the worlds before it were destroyed when wrong was done, so too this Fourth World was destined to be destroyed when the people do not live the right way. That is what the Dine say to this day.

Then the winds went up to the Fourth World.

Fire

The people saw a young woman as beautiful as the sunshine itself.

Nisqually

Pacific Northwest

Loo-Wit, the Fire-Keeper

When the world was young, the Creator gave everyone all that was needed to be happy.

The weather was always pleasant. There was food for everyone and room for all the people. Despite this, though, two brothers began to quarrel over the land. Each wanted to control it. It reached the point where each brother gathered together a group of men to support his claim. Soon it appeared there would be war.

The Creator saw this and was not pleased. He waited until the two brothers were asleep one night and then carried them to a new country. There a beautiful river flowed and tall mountains rose into the clouds. He woke them just as the sun rose and they looked out from the mountaintop to the land below. They saw what a good place it was. It made their hearts good.

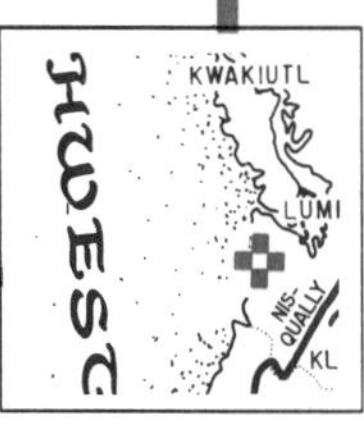

"Now," the Creator said, "this will be your land."

Then he gave each of the brothers a bow and a single arrow. "Shoot your arrow into the air," the Creator said. "Where your arrow falls will be the land of you and your people, and you shall be a great chief there."

The brothers did as they were told. The older brother shot his arrow. It arched over the river and landed to the south in the valley of the Willamette River. There is where he and his people went, and they became the Multnomahs. The younger brother shot his arrow. It flew to the north of the great river. He and his people went there and became the Klickitats.

Then the Creator made a Great Stone Bridge across the river. "This bridge," the Creator said, "is a sign of peace. You and your peoples can visit each other by crossing over this bridge. As long as you remain at peace, as long as your hearts are good, this bridge will stand."

For many seasons the two peoples remained at peace. They passed freely back and forth across the Great Stone Bridge. One day, though, the people to the north looked south toward the Willamette and said, "Their lands are better than ours." One day, though, the people to the south looked north toward the Klickitat and said, "Their lands are more beautiful than ours." Then, once again, the people began to quarrel.

The Creator saw this and was not pleased.

For many seasons the two peoples remained at peace.

The people were becoming greedy again. Their hearts were becoming bad. The Creator darkened the skies and took fire away. Now the people grew cold. The rains of autumn began and the people suffered greatly.

"Give us back fire," they begged. "We wish to live again with each other in peace."

Their prayers reached the Creator's heart. There was only one place on Earth where fire still remained. An old woman named Loo-Wit had stayed out of the quarreling and was not greedy. It was in her lodge only that fire still burned. So the Creator went to Loo-Wit.

"If you will share your fire with all the people," The Creator said, "I will give you whatever you wish. Tell me what you want."

"I want to be young and beautiful," Loo-Wit said.

"That is the way it will be," said the Creator. "Now take your fire to the Great Stone Bridge above the river. Let all the people come to you and get fire. You must keep the fire burning there to remind people that their hearts must stay good."

The next morning, the skies grew clear and the people saw the sun rise for the first time in many days. The sun shone on the Great Stone Bridge and there the people saw a

young woman as beautiful as the sunshine itself.

Before her, there on the bridge, burned a fire. The people came to the fire and ended their quarrels. Loo-Wit gave each of them fire. Now their homes again became warm and peace was everywhere.

One day, though, the chief of the people to the north came to Loo-Wit's fire. He saw how beautiful she was and wanted her to be his wife. At the same time, the chief of the people to the south also saw Loo-Wit's beauty. He, too, wanted to marry her. Loo-Wit could not decide which of the two she liked better. Then the chiefs began to quarrel. Their peoples took up the quarrel and fighting began.

When The Creator saw the fighting he became angry. He broke down the Great Stone Bridge. He took each of the two chiefs and changed them into mountains. The chief of the Klickitats became the mountain we now know as Mount Adams. The chief of the Multnomahs became the mountain we now know as Mount Hood. Even as mountains, they continued to quarrel, throwing flames and stones at each other. In some places, the stones they threw almost blocked the river between them. That is why the Columbia River is so narrow in the place called the Dalles today.

Loo-Wit was heartbroken over the pain caused by her beauty. She no longer wanted to be a beautiful young woman.

She could no longer find peace as a human being.

Loo-Wit was heartbroken over the pain caused by her beauty.

The Creator took pity on her and changed her into a mountain also, the most beautiful of the mountains. She was placed so that she stood between Mount Adams and Mount Hood, and she was allowed to keep the fire within herself which she had once shared on the Great Stone Bridge. Eventually, she became known as Mount St. Helens and she slept peacefully.

Though she was asleep, Loo-Wit was still aware, the people said. The Creator had placed her between the two quarreling mountains to keep the peace, and it was intended that humans, too, should look at her beauty and remember to keep their hearts good, to share the land and treat it well. If we human beings do not treat the land with respect, the people said, Loo-Wit will wake up and let us know how unhappy she and the Creator have become again. So they said long before the day in the 1980s when Mount St. Helens woke again.

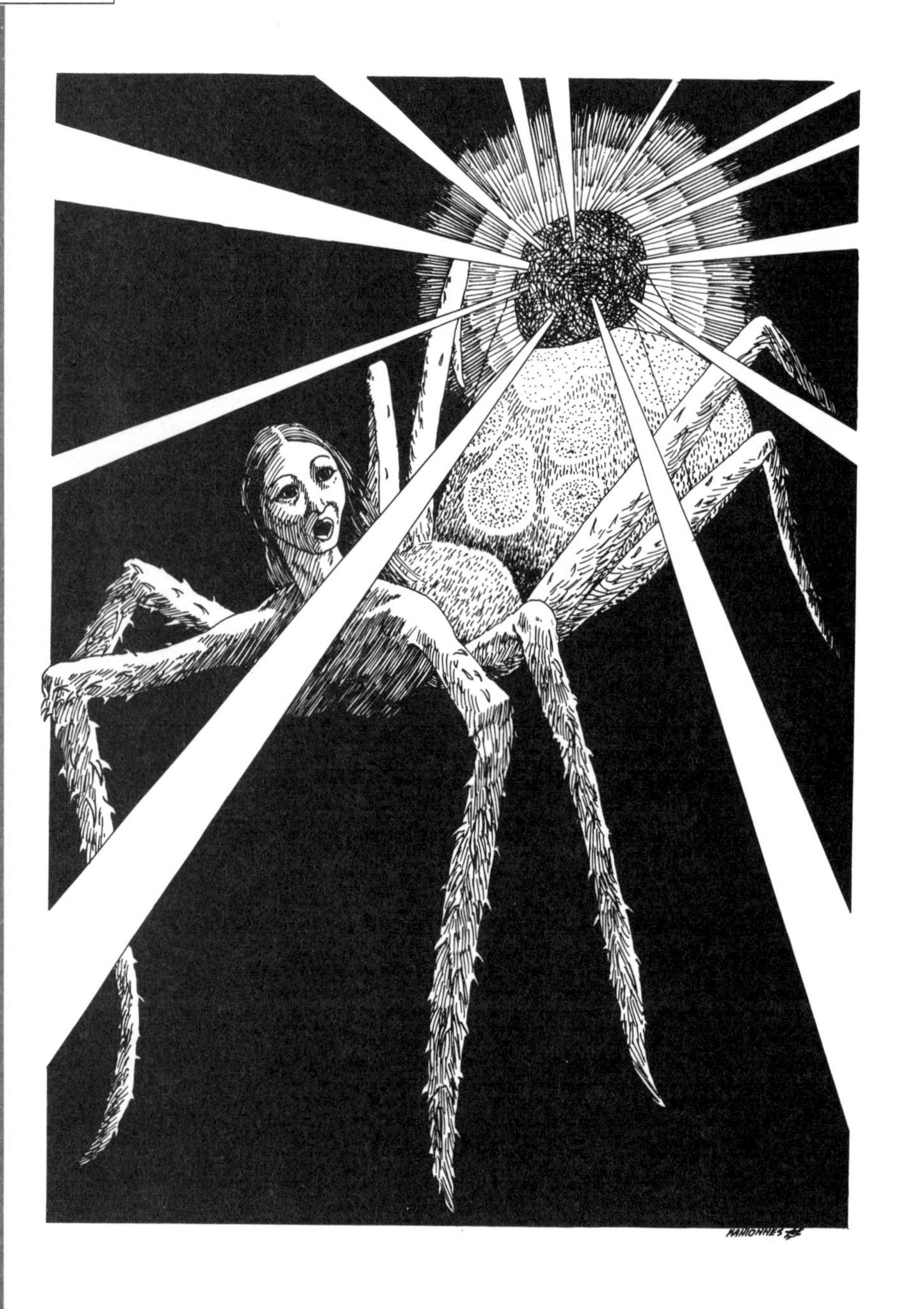

She put the piece of the Sun into her bag and carried it back with her.

Muskogee
[Creek]

Oklahoma

How Grandmother Spider Stole the Sun

When the Earth was first made, there was no light.

It was very hard for the animals and the people in the darkness. Finally, the animals decided to do something about it.

"I have heard there is something called the Sun," said the Bear. "It is kept on the other side of the world, but the people there will not share it. Perhaps we can steal a piece of it."

All the animals agreed that it was a good idea. But who would be the one to steal the Sun?

The Fox was the first to try. He sneaked to the place where the Sun was kept. He waited until no one was looking. Then he grabbed a piece of it in his mouth and ran. But the Sun was so hot it burned his mouth and he dropped it. To this day all foxes have black mouths because that first fox burned his carrying the Sun.

The Possum tried next. In those days, Possum had a very bushy tail. She crept up to the place where the Sun was kept, broke off a piece and hid it in her tail. Then she began to run, bringing the Sun back to the animals and the people. But the Sun was so hot it burned off all the hair on her tail and she lost hold of it. To this day all possums have bare tails because the Sun burned away the hair on that first possum.

Then Grandmother Spider tried. Instead of trying to hold the Sun herself, she wove a bag out of her webbing. She put the piece of the Sun into her bag and carried it back with her. Now the question was where to put the Sun.

Grandmother Spider told them, "The Sun should be up high in the sky. Then everyone will be able to see it and benefit from its light."

All the animals agreed, but none of them could reach up high enough. Even if they carried it to the top of the tallest tree, that would not be high enough for everyone on the Earth to see the Sun. Then they decided to have one of the birds carry the Sun up to the top of the sky. Everyone knew the Buzzard could fly the highest, so he was chosen.

The Buzzard placed the Sun on top of his head, where his feathers were the thickest, for the Sun was still very hot, even inside Grandmother Spider's bag. He began to

Up and up he went, and the Sun grew hotter.

fly, up and up toward the top of the sky. As he flew the Sun grew hotter. Up and up he went, higher and higher, and the Sun grew hotter and hotter still. Now the Sun was burning through Grandmother Spider's bag, but the Buzzard still kept flying up toward the top of the sky. Up and up he went, and the Sun grew hotter. Now it was burning away the feathers on top of his head, but he continued on. Now all of his feathers were gone, but he flew higher. Now it was turning the bare skin of his head all red, but he continued to fly. He flew until he reached the top of the sky, and there he placed the Sun where it would give light to everyone.

Earth

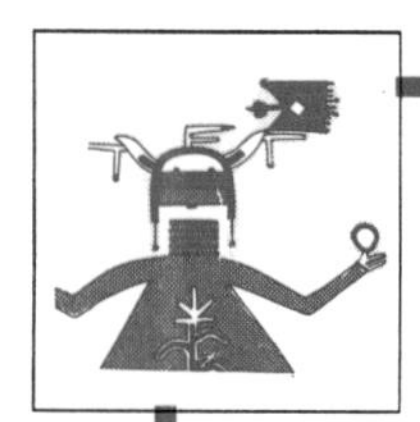

GA-DA-RUM. The big rock was rolling down the hill after Coyote.

Lakota
[Sioux]

Great Plains

Tunka-shila, Grandfather Rock

The Lakota (Sioux) people say that in the beginning everything was in the mind of Wakan-Tanka.

All things which were to be existed only as spirits. Those spirits moved about in space seeking a place to manifest themselves. They traveled until they reached the sun, but it was not a good place for creation to begin because it was too hot. Finally they came to the Earth, which was without life and covered with the great waters. There was no dry land at all for life to begin upon. But then, out of the waters, a great burning rock rose up. It made the dry land appear, and the clouds formed from the steam it created. Then the life on Earth could begin. So it is that the rock is called Tunka-shila, "Grandfather Rock," for it is the oldest one. Because of that, the rocks must be respected. In the sweat lodge, when the water strikes the heated stones and that mist rises once again, it brings back the moment of creation as the people in the lodge sing to Tunka-shila, the Grandfather, the old one.

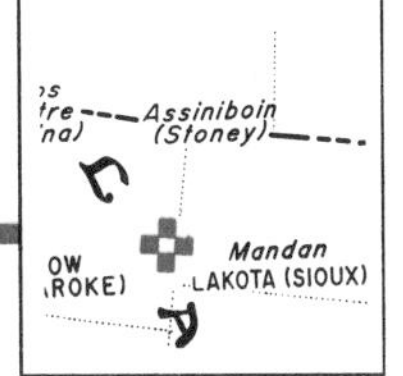

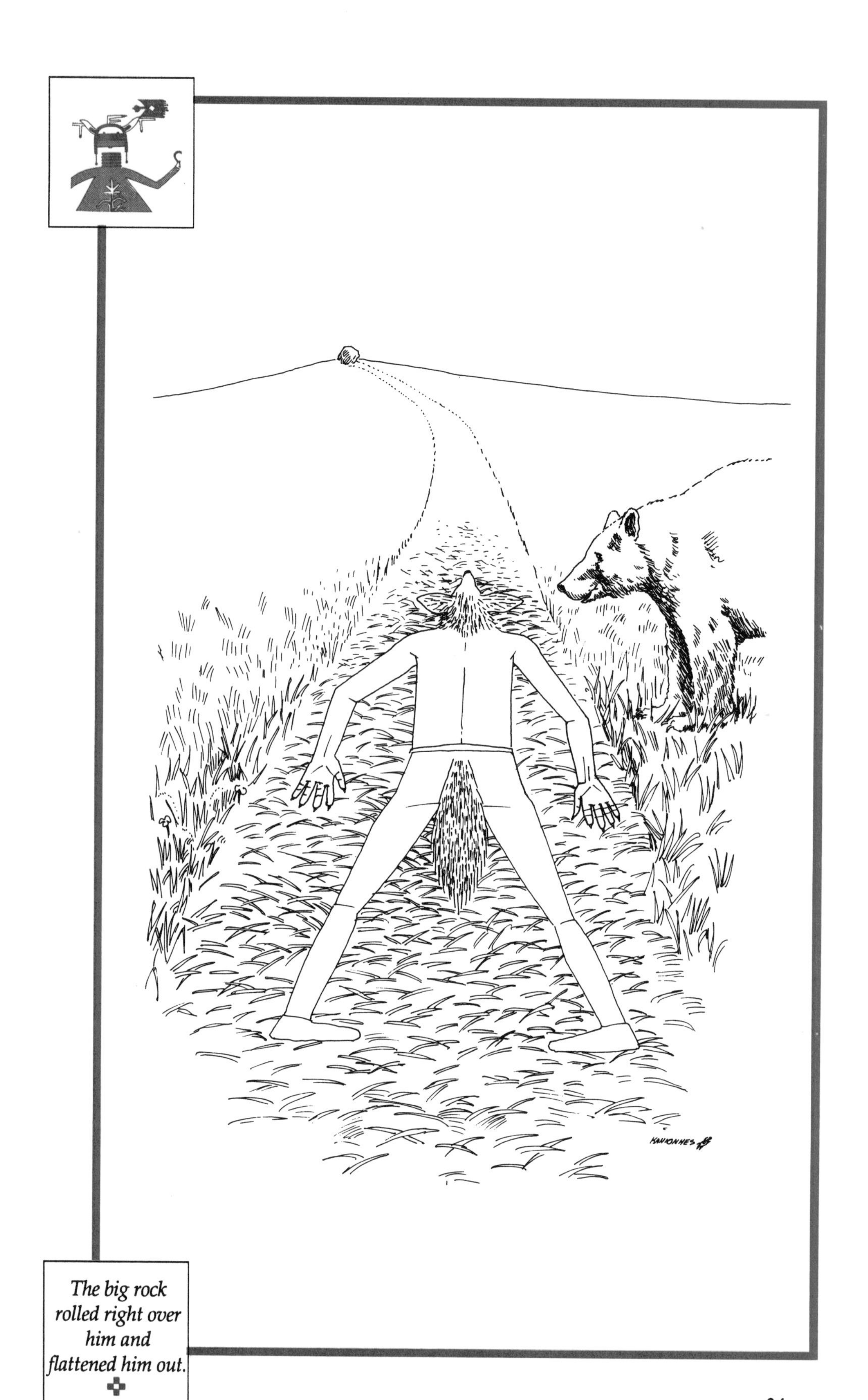

The big rock rolled right over him and flattened him out.

Pawnee

Great Plains

Old Man Coyote and the Rock

Old Man Coyote was going along.

It was quite a while since he had eaten and he was feeling cut in half by hunger. He came to the top of a hill and there he saw a big rock. Old Man Coyote took out his flint knife.

"Grandfather," Old Man Coyote said to the rock, "I give you this fine knife. Now help me in some way, because I am hungry."

Then Old Man Coyote went along further. He went over the top of the hill and there at the bottom was a buffalo that had just been killed.

"How lucky I am," Old Man Coyote said. "But how can I butcher this buffalo without a knife? Now where did I leave my knife?"

Then Old Man Coyote walked back up the hill until

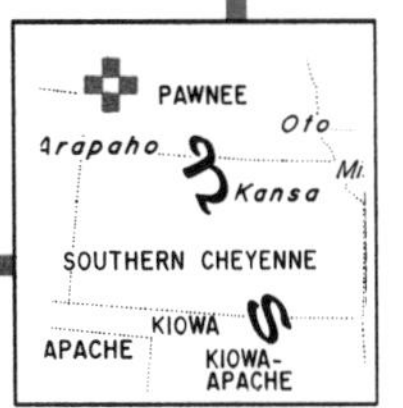

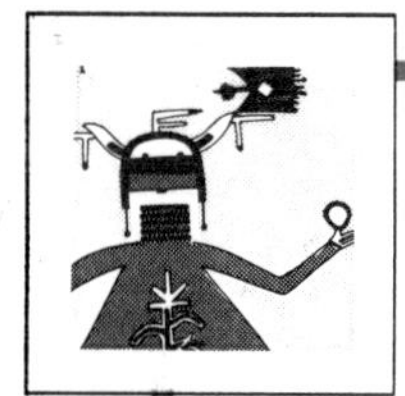

he came to the big rock where his knife still lay on the ground.

"You don't need this knife," he said to the big rock.

Then he picked his flint knife up and ran back to where he had left the buffalo. Now, though, where there had been a freshly killed buffalo, there were only buffalo bones and the bones were very old and gray. Then, from behind him, Old Man Coyote heard a rumbling noise. He turned around and looked up. The big rock was rolling down the hill after him. GA-DA-RUM, GA-DA-RUM.

Old Man Coyote began to run. He ran and ran, but the stone still rumbled after him. GA-DA-RUM, GA-DA-RUM. Old Man Coyote ran until he came to a bear den.

"Help me," he called in to the bears.

The bears looked out and saw what was chasing Old Man Coyote. "We can't help you against Grandfather Rock," they said.

GA-DA-RUM, GA-DA-RUM. The big rock kept coming and Old Man Coyote kept running. Now he came to a cave where the mountain lions lived and he called out again.

"Help me," Old Man Coyote said. "I am about to be killed!"

The big rock kept coming and Old Man Coyote kept running.

The mountain lions looked out and saw what was after Old Man Coyote. "No," they said, "we can't help you if you have angered Grandfather Rock."

GA-DA-RUM, GA-DA-RUM. The big rock kept rumbling after Old Man Coyote and he kept running. Now he came to the place where a bull buffalo was grazing.

"Help me," Old Man Coyote yelled. "That big rock said it was going to kill all the buffalo. When I tried to stop it, it began to chase me."

The bull buffalo braced his legs and thrust his head out to stop the big rock. But the rock just brushed the bull buffalo aside and left him standing there dazed, with his horns bent and his head pushed back into his shoulders. To this day all buffalo are still like that.

GA-DA-RUM, GA-DA-RUM. The big rock kept rolling and Old Man Coyote kept running. But Old Man Coyote was getting tired now and the rock was getting closer. Then Old Man Coyote looked up and saw a nighthawk flying overhead.

"My friend," Old Man Coyote yelled up to the nighthawk, "this big rock that is chasing me said you are ugly. It said you have a wide mouth and your eyes are too big and your beak is all pinched up. I told it not to say that and it began to chase me."

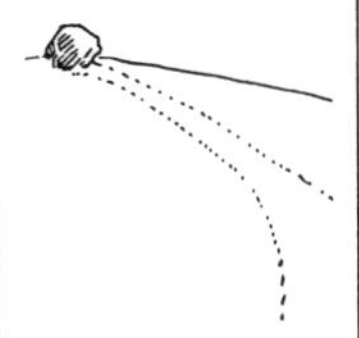

The nighthawk heard what Old Man Coyote said and grew very angry. He called the other nighthawks. They began to swoop down and strike at the big rock with their beaks. Each time they struck the big rock a piece broke off and stopped rolling. GA-DA-RUM, GA-DA-RUM. The rock kept rolling and Old Man Coyote kept running, but now the rock was much smaller. The nighthawks continued to swoop down and break off pieces. Finally the big rock was nothing but small pebbles.

Old Man Coyote came up and looked at the little stones. "My, my," he said to the nighthawks, "Why did you wide-mouthed, big-eyed, pinch-beaked birds do that to my old friend?" Then Old Man Coyote laughed and started on his way again.

Now the nighthawks were very angry at Old Man Coyote. They gathered all of the pieces of the big rock and fanned them together with their wings. The next thing Old Man Coyote knew, he heard a familiar sound behind him again. GA-DA-RUM, GA-DA-RUM. He tried to run, but he was so tired now he could not get away. The big rock rolled right over him and flattened him out.

The bears looked out and saw what was chasing Old Man Coyote.

Wind and Weather

He had to pull himself along by grabbing hold of the boulders.

Abenaki

Northeast Woodlands

Gluscabi and the Wind Eagle

Long ago, Gluscabi lived with his grandmother, Woodchuck, in a small lodge beside the big water.

One day Gluscabi was walking around when he looked out and saw some ducks in the bay.

"I think it is time to go hunt some ducks," he said. So he took his bow and arrows and got into his canoe. He began to paddle out into the bay and as he paddled he sang:

Ki yo wah ji neh
yo ho hey ho
Ki yo wah ji neh
Ki yo wah ji neh.

But a wind came up and it turned his canoe and blew him back to shore. Once again Gluscabi began to paddle out and this time he sang his song a little harder:

KI YO WAH JI NEH
YO HO HEY HO
KI YO WAH JI NEH
KI YO WAH JI NEH.

But again the wind came and blew him back to shore.

Four times he tried to paddle out into the bay and four times he failed. He was not happy. He went back to the lodge of his grandmother and walked right in, even though there was a stick leaning across the door, which meant that the person inside was doing some work and did not want to be disturbed.

"Grandmother," Gluscabi said, "What makes the wind blow?"

Grandmother Woodchuck looked up from her work. "Gluscabi," she said, "Why do you want to know?"

Then Gluscabi answered her just as every child in the world does when they are asked such a question.

"Because," he said.

Grandmother Woodchuck looked at him. "Ah, Gluscabi," she said. "Whenever you ask such questions I feel there is going to be trouble. And perhaps I should not tell you. But I know that you are so stubborn you will never stop asking until I answer you. So I shall tell you. Far from here, on top of the tallest mountain, a great bird stands. This bird is named Wuchowsen, and when he flaps his wings he makes the wind blow."

"Eh-hey, Grandmother," said Gluscabi, "I see. Now how would one find that place where the Wind Eagle stands?"

Far from here, on top of the tallest mountain, a great bird stands.

Again Grandmother Woodchuck looked at Gluscabi. "Ah, Gluscabi," she said, "Once again I feel that perhaps I should not tell you. But I know that you are very stubborn and would never stop asking. So, I shall tell you. If you walk always facing the wind you will come to the place where Wuchowsen stands."

"Thank you, Grandmother," said Gluscabi. He stepped out of the lodge and faced into the wind and began to walk.

He walked across the fields and through the woods and the wind blew hard. He walked through the valleys and into the hills and the wind blew harder still. He came to the foothills and began to climb and the wind still blew harder. Now the foothills were becoming mountains and the

wind was very strong. Soon there were no longer any trees and the wind was very, very strong. The wind was so strong that it blew off Gluscabi's moccasins. But he was very stubborn and he kept on walking, leaning into the wind. Now the wind was so strong that it blew off his shirt, but he kept on walking. Now the wind was so strong that it blew off all his clothes and he was naked, but he still kept walking. Now the wind was so strong that it blew off his hair, but Gluscabi still kept walking, facing into the wind. The wind was so strong that it blew off his eyebrows, but still he continued to walk. Now the wind was so strong that he could hardly stand. He had to pull himself along by grabbing hold of the boulders. But there, on the peak ahead of him, he could see a great bird slowly flapping its wings. It was Wuchowsen, the Wind Eagle.

Gluscabi took a deep breath. "GRANDFATHER!" he shouted.

The Wind Eagle stopped flapping his wings and looked around. "Who calls me Grandfather?" he said.

Gluscabi stood up. "It's me, Grandfather. I just came up here to tell you that you do a very good job making the wind blow."

The Wind Eagle puffed out his chest with pride. "You mean like this?" he said and flapped his wings even harder. The wind which he made was so strong that it lifted

The Wind Eagle stopped flapping his wings and looked around.

Gluscabi right off his feet, and he would have been blown right off the mountain had he not reached out and grabbed a boulder again.

"GRANDFATHER!!!" Gluscabi shouted again.

The Wind Eagle stopped flapping his wings. "Yesss?" he said.

Gluscabi stood up and came closer to Wuchowsen. "You do a very good job of making the wind blow, Grandfather. This is so. But it seems to me that you could do an even better job if you were on that peak over there."

The Wind Eagle looked toward the other peak. "That may be so," he said, "but how would I get from here to there?"

Gluscabi smiled. "Grandfather," he said, "I will carry you. Wait here." Then Gluscabi ran back down the mountain until he came to a big basswood tree. He stripped off the outer bark and from the inner bark he braided a strong carrying strap which he took back up the mountain to the Wind Eagle. "Here, Grandfather," he said. "let me wrap this around you so I can lift you more easily." Then he wrapped the carrying strap so tightly around Wuchowsen that his wings were pulled in to his sides and he could hardly breathe. "Now, Grandfather," Gluscabi said, picking the Wind Eagle up, "I will take you to a better place." He began to walk toward the other peak, but as

he walked he came to a place where there was a large crevice, and as he stepped over it he let go of the carrying strap and the Wind Eagle slid down into the crevice, upside down, and was stuck.

"Now," Gluscabi said, "It is time to hunt some ducks."

He walked back down the mountain and there was no wind at all. He walked till he came to the treeline and still no wind blew. He walked down to the foothills and down to the hills and the valleys and still there was no wind. He walked through the forests and through the fields, and the wind did not blow at all. He walked and walked until he came back to the lodge by the water, and by now all his hair had grown back. He put on some fine new clothing and a new pair of moccasins and took his bow and arrows and went down to the bay and climbed into his boat to hunt ducks. He paddled out into the water and sang his canoeing song:

Ki yo wah ji neh
yo ho hey ho
Ki yo wah ji neh
Ki yo wah ji neh.

But the air was very hot and still and he began to sweat. The air was so still and hot that it was hard to breathe. Soon the water began to grow dirty and smell bad and there was so much foam on the water he could hardly paddle. He was not pleased at all and he returned to the shore and went straight to his grandmother's lodge and walked in.

He paddled out into the water and sang his canoeing song.

"Grandmother," he said, "What is wrong? The air is hot and still and it is making me sweat and it is hard to breathe. The water is dirty and covered with foam. I cannot hunt ducks at all like this."

Grandmother Woodchuck looked up at Gluscabi. "Gluscabi," she said, "what have you done now?"

And Gluscabi answered just as every child in the world answers when asked that question, "Oh, nothing," he said.

"Gluscabi," said Grandmother Woodchuck again, "Tell me what you have done."

Then Gluscabi told her about going to visit the Wind Eagle and what he had done to stop the wind.

"Oh, Gluscabi," said Grandmother Woodchuck, "will you never learn? Tabaldak, The Owner, set the Wind Eagle on that mountain to make the wind because we need the wind. The wind keeps the air cool and clean. The wind brings the clouds which gives us rain to wash the Earth. The wind moves the waters and keeps them fresh and sweet. Without the wind, life will not be good for us, for our children or our children's children."

Gluscabi nodded his head. "Kaamoji, Grandmother," he said. "I understand."

Then he went outside. He faced in the direction from which the wind had once come and began to walk. He walked through the fields and through the forests and the wind did not blow and he felt very hot. He walked through the valleys and up the hills and there was no wind and it was hard for him to breathe. He came to the foothills and began to climb and he was very hot and sweaty indeed. At last he came to the mountain where the Wind Eagle once stood and he went and looked down into the crevice. There was Wuchowsen, the Wind Eagle, wedged upside down.

"Uncle?" Gluscabi called.

The Wind Eagle looked up as best he could. "Who calls me Uncle?" he said.

"It is Gluscabi, Uncle. I'm up here. But what are you doing down there?"

"Oh, Gluscabi," said the Wind Eagle, "a very ugly naked man with no hair told me that he would take me to the other peak so that I could do a better job of making the wind blow. He tied my wings and picked me up, but as he stepped over this crevice he dropped me in and I am stuck. And I am not comfortable here at all."

"Ah, Grandfath . . . er, Uncle, I will get you out."

The wind brings the clouds which gives us rain to wash the Earth.

Then Gluscabi climbed down into the crevice. He pulled the Wind Eagle free and placed him back on his mountain and untied his wings.

"Uncle," Gluscabi said, "It is good that the wind should blow sometimes and other times it is good that it should be still."

The Wind Eagle looked at Gluscabi and then nodded his head. "Grandson," he said, "I hear what you say."

So it is that sometimes there is wind and sometimes it is still to this very day. And so the story goes.

Water

"Let me go ahead of you," said Grandmother Spider.

The Hero Twins and the Swallower of Clouds

To the American Indian people of the dry Southwest, few things are more important than rain.

The people speak of different kinds of rain: the *male rain,* which strikes hard on the Earth and washes away; the *female rain,* which falls gently and steadily, soaking the soil. Many stories are told of the rain, and songs relate to the coming of the rain. One of the corn-grinding songs of the Zuni people praises the mountains, from which the clouds come:

> Clouds come rising out of my beautiful mountain.
> Up in the sky, the rain makers are sitting.
> One after another rain clouds are coming.
> Over there the flowers are coming.
> Here the young corn is growing.

The clouds are powerful and benevolent, connected to the kachinas, those helping spirits of the ancestors. So when the Zuni tell the story of the giant, Swallower of Clouds, they tell of a very terrible monster indeed.

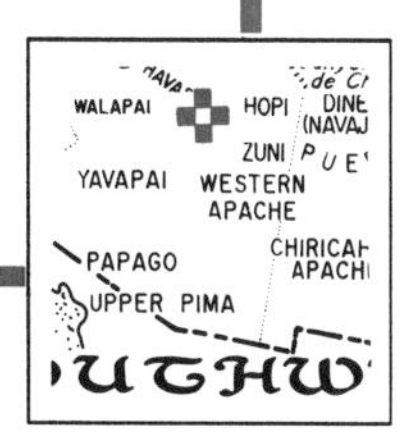

When the world was young, they say, a giant lived in the cliffs above Cañon de Chelly. The food he lived on was human beings, and he caught the clouds and squeezed them into his mouth for drink. The people called him Swallower of Clouds, and the bravest of the men tried to destroy him. However, anyone who went out to kill the giant was never seen again. Before long, because he was swallowing all the clouds, the snow stopped falling to the north. Because he was swallowing all the clouds, the rain no longer came from the west. Because he was swallowing all the clouds, the mist above the mountains to the east disappeared. Because he was swallowing all the clouds, the springs to the south dried up. The crops dried up and died. The people were suffering and some began to die.

The Hero Twins saw what was happening.

"We will go and kill Swallower of Clouds," they said. Then they started on their way to the cliffs where he lived. But as they were following the path to the cliffs, they saw a spider web next to the trail.

"Grandmother Spider," they said, greeting the maker of webs, "Are you well?"

"I am well, Grandchildren," said the spider. "Where are you going?"

"We are going to kill the giant, Swallower of Clouds," they said.

The giant has a trick. He stretches himself out on top of the cliffs.

"That is good," Grandmother Spider said, "but first let me warn you. The giant has a trick. He stretches himself out on top of the cliffs. He pretends to be sleeping and then tells whoever comes to pass under his legs, which are arched over the trail. As soon as someone passes under, though, he grabs them and throws them over the cliff."

"Grandmother," said the Hero Twins, "what should we do?"

"Let me go ahead of you," said Grandmother Spider. "Wait for a while and then follow." Then Grandmother Spider set out. She did not go far before she came to the giant. He was stretched out on top of the cliff with his legs over the trail. He was as huge as a hill and his legs were bigger than tree trunks. He pretended to sleep, for he had heard the Hero Twins were coming to fight him. Grandmother Spider, though, was so small the giant did not see her. She climbed up a rock behind him and then let herself down on his forehead with a strand of silk. While he kept his eyes closed, pretending to sleep, she wove her web across his eyes so that he could not open them up.

Now the Hero Twins, having waited for a while, started on their way. When they came close to the place where Swallower of Clouds lay, they began to sing a war song.

"Who is that?" said Swallower of Clouds as the Hero Twins came closer, "I am old and tired, too old and tired to move out of the way. Just pass under my legs."

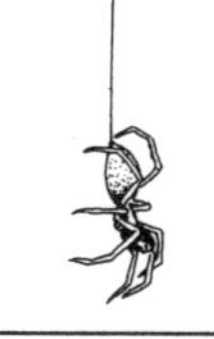

Anyone who went out to kill the giant was never seen again.

But when the Hero Twins came close to the giant, they split up. One ran to the right and one ran to the left. The giant tried to open his eyes to see what they were doing, but he was blinded by the spider web.

"Where are you, Little Ones?" he said, striking at them and missing. "Just pass under my legs."

Swallower of Clouds struck again at the Hero Twins, but he could not see them and he missed. Then the Twins leaped up and struck him with their clubs. One struck him in the head. The other struck him in the stomach. They killed Swallower of Clouds with their clubs. Then they threw him over the same cliffs where he had thrown all the people he had killed. Now the clouds were able to pass again through the mountains. The snow returned to the north. The rain came again from the west. The mists formed once more above the mountains to the east. The springs to the south flowed once more. Again the crops of the people grew and the people were well and happy.

It is said that when the giant fell, he struck so hard that his feet drove into the Earth. He still stands there to this day with his blood dried red all along his great stiff body. Though some call that great stone by other names, the Zunis know it is the Swallower of Clouds. When they see it they are thankful for the deed of the Hero Twins and the life-giving rain.

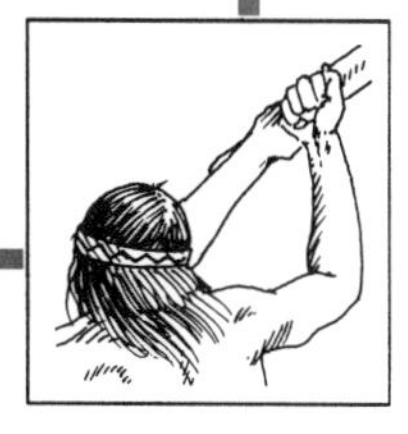

Half of his face was painted black and half was painted white.

Micmac and Maliseet

✣

Maritime Provinces

Koluscap and the Water Monster

Once there was a great drought.

The rain stopped falling and the Earth became dry. Finally, the streams themselves stopped flowing. There was a village of people who lived by the side of a stream, and life now became very hard for them. They sent someone upstream to see why the stream had stopped. Before long, the man came back.

"There is a dam across the stream," he said. "It is holding back all the water. There are guards on the dam. They say their chief is keeping all the water for himself."

"Go and beg him for water," said the elders of the village. "Tell him we are dying without water to drink." So the messenger went back again. When he returned, he held a bark cup filled with mud.

"This is all the water their chief will allow us to have," he said.

Now the people were angry. They decided to fight.

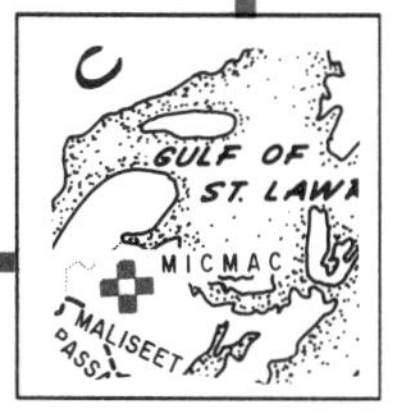

They sent a party of warriors to destroy the dam. But as soon as the warriors came to the dam, a great monster rose out of the water. His mouth was big enough to swallow a moose. His belly was huge and yellow. He grabbed the warriors and crushed them in his long fingers which were like the roots of cedar trees. Only one warrior escaped to come back to the people and tell them what happened.

"We cannot fight a monster," the people said. They were not sure what to do. Then one of the old chiefs spoke. "We must pray to Gitchee Manitou," he said. "Perhaps he will pity us and send help." Then they burned tobacco and sent their prayers up to the Creator.

Their prayers were heard. Gitchee Manitou looked down and saw the people were in great trouble. He decided to take pity and help them and he called Koluscap. "Go and help the people," Gitchee Manitou said.

Koluscap then went down to the Earth. He took the shape of a tall warrior, head and shoulders taller than any of the people. Half of his face was painted black and half was painted white. A great eagle perched on his right shoulder and by his side two wolves walked as his dogs, a black wolf and a white wolf. As soon as the people saw him they welcomed him. They thought surely he was someone sent by the Creator to help them.

"We cannot afford you anything to drink," they said.

As soon as the people saw him they welcomed him.

"All the water in the world is kept by the monster and his dam."

"Where is this monster?" Koluscap said, swinging his war club, which was made of the root of a birch tree.

"Up the dry stream bed," they said.

So Koluscap walked up the dry stream bed. As he walked he saw dried up and dead fish and turtles and other water animals. Soon he came to the dam, which stretched between two hills.

"I have come for water," he said to the guards on top of the dam.

"GIVE HIM NONE, GIVE HIM NONE!" said a big voice from the other side of the dam. So the guards did not give him water.

Again Koluscap asked and again the big voice answered. Four times he made his request, and on the fourth request Koluscap was thrown a bark cup half-full of filthy water.

Then Koluscap grew angry. He stomped his foot and the dam began to crack. He stomped his foot again and he began to grow taller and taller. Now Koluscap was taller than the dam, taller even than the monster who sat in the deep water.

Koluscap's club was now bigger than a great pine tree. He struck the dam with his club and the dam burst open and the water flowed out.

Then he reached down and grabbed the water monster. It tried to fight back, but Koluscap was too powerful. With one giant hand Koluscap squeezed the water monster and its eyes bulged out and its back grew bent. He rubbed it with his other hand and it grew smaller and smaller.

"Now," Koluscap said, "no longer will you keep others from having water. Now you'll just be a bullfrog. But I will take pity on you and you can live in this water from now on." Then Koluscap threw the water monster back into the stream. To this day, even though he hides from everyone because Koluscap frightened him so much, you may still hear the bullfrog saying, "Give Him None, Give Him None."

The water flowed past the village. Some of the people were so happy to see the water that they jumped into the stream. They dove so deep and stayed in so long that they became fish and water creatures themselves. They still live in that river today, sharing the water which no one person can ever own.

It tried to fight back, but Koluscap was too powerful.

Yurok

California

How Thunder and Earthquake Made Ocean

Thunder lived at Sumig.

One day he said, "How shall the people live if there is just prairie there? Let us place the ocean there." He said to Earthquake, "I want to have water there, there so that the people may live. Otherwise they will have nothing to live on." He said to Earthquake, "What do you think?"

Earthquake thought. "That is true," he said. "There should be water there. Far off I see it. I see the water. It is at Opis. There are salmon there and water."

"Go," said Thunder. "Go with Kingfisher, the one who sits there by the water. Go and get water at Opis. Get the water that is to come here."

Then the two of them went. Kingfisher and Earthquake went to see the water. They went to get the water at Opis. They had two abalone shells that Thunder had given

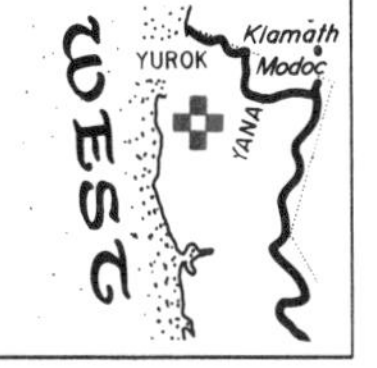

They had two abalone shells that Thunder had given to them.

to them. "Take these shells," Thunder had said. "Collect the water in them."

First Kingfisher and Earthquake went to the north end of the world. There Earthquake looked around. "This will be easy," he said. "It will be easy for me to sink this land." Then Earthquake ran around. He ran around and the ground sank. It sank there at the north end of the world.

Then Kingfisher and Earthquake started for Opis. They went to the place at the end of the water. They made the ground sink behind them as they went. At Opis they saw all kinds of seals and salmon. They saw all the kinds of animals and fish that could be eaten there in the water at Opis. Then they took water in the abalone shells.

"Now we will go to the south end of the world," said Earthquake. "We will go there and look at the water. Thunder, who is at Sumig, will help us by breaking down the trees. The water will extend all the way to the south end of the world. There will be salmon and fish of all kinds and seals in the water."

Now Kingfisher and Earthquake came back to Sumig. They saw that Thunder had broken down the trees. Together the three of them went north. As they went together they kept sinking the ground. The Earth quaked and quaked and water flowed over it as Kingfisher and Earthquake poured it from their abalone shells. Kingfisher emptied his shell and it filled the ocean halfway to the north end of the world. Earthquake emptied his shell and it filled the ocean the rest of the way.

As they filled in the ocean, the creatures which would be food swarmed into the water. The seals came as if they were thrown in in handfuls. Into the water they came, swimming toward shore. Earthquake sank the land deeper to make gullies and the whales came swimming through the gullies where the water was deep enough for them to travel. The salmon came running through the water.

Now all the land animals, the deer and elk, the foxes and mink, the bear and others had gone inland. Now the water creatures were there. Now Thunder and Kingfisher and Earthquake looked at the ocean. "This is enough," they said. "Now the people will have enough to live on. Everything that is needed is in the water."

So it is that the prairie became ocean. It is so because Thunder wished it so. It is so because Earthquake wished it so. All kinds of creatures are in the ocean before us because Thunder and Earthquake wished the people to live.

"Everything that is needed is in the water."

Inuit

Arctic Regions

Sedna, the Woman Under the Sea

Long ago an Inung man and his daughter, Sedna, lived together along the ocean.

Their life was not easy, for the fishing was often not good and the hunting was often poor. Still, Sedna grew up to be a strong and handsome young woman and many Inung men came to ask her to marry. No one, though, was good enough for her. She was too proud to accept any of them. One day, just at the time when the long days were beginning and the ice was breaking for spring, a handsome man came to Sedna. He wore clothing of grey and white and Sedna could see that he was not like other men. He was a sea-bird, the fulmar, taking the shape of a man to woo her and he sang to her this song:

Come with me, come with me
to the land of the birds
where there never is hunger,
you shall rest on soft bearskins.

Come with me, come with me
to my beautiful tent,
my fellow birds will bring you
all that your heart desires.

Sedna grasped the side of the boat. "Let go," Aja shouted at her.

Come with me, come with me
and our feathers will clothe you,
your lamp will be filled with oil,
your pot will be filled with meat.

His song was so lovely and his promises so enticing that Sedna could not resist him. She agreed to go with him, off across the wide sea. Their journey to his land was a long and hard one. When they reached the place where the fulmar lived, Sedna saw that he had deceived her. His tent was not beautiful and covered with soft skins. It was made of fishskins and full of holes so that wind and snow blew in. Her bed was not made of soft bearskins, but of hard walrus hide. There was no oil for her lamp, for there were no lamps at all, and her food was nothing but raw fish. Too late, Sedna realized the mistake she had made and she sang this song:

Aja, my father, if only you knew
how wretched I am, you would come to me.
Aja, my father, we would hurry away
in your boat across the wide sea.

The birds do not look kindly
on me, for I am a stranger.
Cold winds blow about my bed
and I have little food.

Aja, my father, come and take me back home.

So she sang each day as a year passed. Now the ice broke again and Aja decided he would go and visit his daughter. In his swift boat he crossed the wide sea and came to the fulmar's country. He found his daughter, cold and hungry, in a small tent made only of fishskins. She greeted him with joy, begging him to take her back home. Just then, the fulmar returned from fishing. Aja was so angry that he struck the fulmar with his knife and killed him.

Then he placed Sedna in his boat and began to paddle swiftly back across the sea.

Soon the other fulmars came back from fishing. They found the body of Sedna's husband and they began to cry. To this day you can still hear the fulmars mourning and crying as they fly over the sea. They decided to find the one who had killed their brother and they began to fly in great circles over the sea, searching him out.

Before long, they saw the boat of Aja. They saw Sedna was with him and knew that he was the one who was the murderer. Then, using their magical powers, the fulmars made a great storm begin. The waves lifted high above the small boat and Aja became very afraid. He had seen the birds and knew that they were causing the storm to punish him for the death of Sedna's husband.

"You fulmars," he cried, "look! I give you back this girl. Do not kill me." Then he pushed his daughter out of the boat. But Sedna grasped the side of the boat.

"Let go," Aja shouted at her. "The fulmars will kill me if I do not give you to the sea." But Sedna still held on to the side of the boat. Then, taking his sharp knife, Aja cut off the tips of her fingers. The ends of her fingers fell into the water and became the whales. Sedna still grasped the side of the boat and now her father cut off the middle joints of her fingers. Those, too, fell into the water and were transformed into seals.

The waves lifted high above the small boat and Aja became very afraid.

The fulmars, who saw what Aja did, thought it certain that Sedna would drown. They were satisfied and flew away. As soon as they departed, the storm ended and Aja pulled his daughter back into the boat.

Now, though, Sedna hated her father. When they had reached shore and her father had gone to sleep in his tent, she called to her dogs, who would do whatever she said. "Gnaw off the hands and feet of my father," she said. And the dogs did as she said. When this happened, Aja cursed his daughter. The Earth opened beneath them and all of them fell deep down to the land of Adlivun, which is beneath the land and the sea.

To this day, that is where Sedna lives. Because the whales and the seals were made from her fingers, she can call them and tell them where to go. So it is that when the people wish to hunt, they have their *angakok*, the shaman, descend in his dream-trance to the land under the sea where Sedna lives.

He combs out Sedna's long, tangled hair, for without fingers she is unable to do it herself. Then he can ask her to send the whales and seals back to the places where the people can hunt them. Thanks to the blessings of Sedna, who is always generous to those who remember to ask her help in the right way, the people no longer go hungry.

There she sat, the tide-line held firmly in her hand.

Tsimshian

Pacific Northwest

How Raven Made the Tides

A long time ago, the old people say, the tide did not come in or go out.

The ocean would stay very high up on the shore for a long time and the clams and the seaweed and the other good things to eat would be hidden under the deep water. The people were often hungry.

"This is not the way it should be," said Raven. Then he put on his blanket of black feathers and flew along the coast, following the line of the tide. At last he came to the house of a very old woman who was the one who held the tide-line in her hand. As long as she held onto it the tide would stay high. Raven walked into the old woman's house. There she sat, the tide-line held firmly in her hand. Raven sat down across from her.

"Ah," he said, "Those clams were good to eat."

"What clams?" said the old woman.

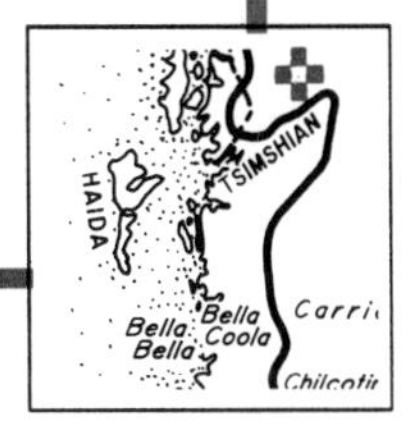

But Raven did not answer her. Instead he patted his stomach and said, "Ah, it was so easy to pick them up that I have eaten as much as I can eat."

"That can't be so," said the old woman, trying to look past Raven to see out her door, but Raven blocked the entrance. So she stood up and leaned past him to look out. Then Raven pushed her so that she fell through the door, and as she fell he threw dust into her eyes so that she was blinded. She let go of the tide-line then and the tide rushed out, leaving all kinds of clams and crabs and other good things to eat exposed.

Raven went out and began to gather clams. He gathered as much as he could carry and ate until he could eat no more. All along the beach others were gathering the good food and thanking Raven for what he had done. Finally he came back to the place where the old woman still was. "Raven," she said, "I know it is you. Heal my eyes so that I can see again."

"I will heal you," Raven said, "but only if you promise to let go of the tide-line twice a day. The people cannot wait so long to gather food from the beaches."

"I will do it," said the old woman. Then Raven washed out her eyes and she could see again. So it is that the tide comes in and goes out every day because Raven made the old woman let go of the tide-line.

Finally he came back to the place where the old woman still was.

Sky

"Take Coyote
out of the sky,"
they said.

Kalispel

Idaho

How Coyote Was the Moon

A long time ago there was no moon.

The people got tired of going around at night in the dark. There had been a moon before, but someone stole it. So they gathered together and talked about it.

"We need to have a moon," they said. "Who will be the moon?"

"I will do it," said Yellow Fox. They placed him in the sky. But he shone so brightly that he made things hot at night. Thus they had to take him down.

Then the people went to Coyote. "Would you like to be the moon? Do you think you could do a better job?"

"I sure would," Coyote said. Then he smiled. He knew that if he became the moon he could look down and see everything that was happening on Earth.

They placed Coyote up in the sky. He did not make the nights too hot and bright. For a time the people were pleased.

"Coyote is doing a good job as the moon," they agreed.

But Coyote, up there in the sky, could see everything that was happening on Earth. He could see whenever someone did something they were not supposed to do and he just couldn't keep quiet.

"Hey," he would shout, so loudly everyone on Earth could hear him, "that man is stealing meat from the drying racks." He would look down over people's shoulders as they played games in the moonlight. "Hey," he would shout, "that person there is cheating at the moccasin game."

Finally, all the people who wished to do things in secret got together. "Take Coyote out of the sky," they said. "He is making too much noise with all of his shouting."

So Coyote was taken out of the sky. Someone else became the moon. Coyote could no longer see what everyone on Earth was doing, but that hasn't stopped him from still trying to snoop into everyone else's business ever since.

Someone else became the moon.

Anishinabe

Great Lakes Region

How Fisher Went to the Skyland: The Origin of the Big Dipper

Fisher was a great hunter.

He was not big, but he was known for his determination and was regarded as one with great power. Fisher's son wanted to be a great hunter also. One day the son went out to try to catch something. It was not easy, for the snow was very deep and it was very cold everywhere. In those days it was always winter on the Earth and there was no such thing as warm weather. The son hunted a long time with no luck. Finally, though, he saw a squirrel. As quietly as he could he sneaked up and then pounced, catching the squirrel between his paws. Before he could kill it, though, the squirrel spoke to him.

"Grandson," said the squirrel, "don't kill me. I can give you some good advice."

"Speak then," said the young fisher.

"I see that you are shivering from the cold.

"Grandson," said the squirrel, "don't kill me. I can give you some good advice."

If you do what I tell you, we may all enjoy warm weather. Then it will be easy for all of us to find food and not starve as we are doing now."

"Tell me what to do, Grandfather," the young fisher said, letting the squirrel go.

The squirrel climbed quickly up onto a high branch and then spoke again. "Go home and say nothing. Just sit down in your lodge and begin to weep. Your mother will ask you what is wrong, but you must not answer her. If she tries to comfort you or give you food, you must refuse it. When your father comes home, he will ask you why you are weeping. Then you can speak. Tell him the winds are too cold and the snow is too deep. Tell him that he must bring warm weather to the Earth."

So the young fisher went home. He sat in the corner of the lodge and cried. His mother asked what was wrong, but he did not answer. She offered him food, but he pushed it away. When his father returned and saw his only son weeping, he went to his side.

"What is wrong, son?" Fisher said. Then the young fisher said what the squirrel had told him to say.

"I am weeping because the wind is too cold and the snow is too deep. We are all starving because of the winter. I want you to use your powers to bring the warm weather."

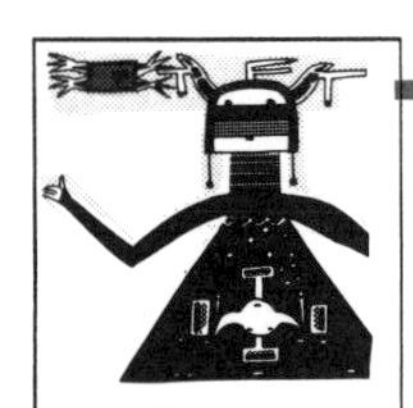

But Fisher never struck the Earth.

"The thing you are asking of me is hard to do," said Fisher, "but you are right. I will do all I can to grant your wish."

Then Fisher had a great feast. He invited all of his friends and told them what he planned to do.

"I am going to go to the place where the skyland is closest to the Earth," he said. "There in the skyland the people have all the warm weather. I intend to go there to bring some of that warm weather back. Then the snow will go away and we will have plenty to eat."

All of Fisher's friends were pleased and offered to go with him. So when Fisher set out, he took the strongest of his friends along. Those friends were Otter, Lynx and Wolverine.

The four of them traveled for a long time through the snow. They went toward the mountains, higher and higher each day. Fisher had with him a pack filled with dried venison and they slept at night buried under the snow. At last, after many, many days, they came to the highest mountain and climbed to its top. Then Fisher took a pipe and tobacco out of his pouch.

"We must offer our smoke to the Four Directions," Fisher said. The four of them smoked and sent their prayers to Gitchee Manitou, asking for success. The sky was very close above them, but they had to find some way to break through into the land above. "We must jump up," said Fisher. "Who will go first?"

"I will try," said Otter. He leaped up and struck the sky but did not break through. Instead he fell back and slid on his belly all the way to the bottom of the mountain. To this day all otters slide like that in the snow.

"Now it is my turn," said Lynx. He jumped too, striking hard against the sky and falling back unconscious. Fisher tried then, but even he did not have enough power.

"Now it is your turn," said Fisher to Wolverine. "You are the strongest of us all."

Wolverine leaped. He struck hard against the sky and fell back, but he did not give up. He leaped again and again until he had made a crack in the sky. Once more he leaped and finally broke through. Fisher jumped through the hole in the sky after him.

The skyland was a beautiful place. It was warm and sunny, and there were plants and flowers of all kinds growing. They could hear the singing of birds all around them, but they could see no people. They went farther and found many long lodges. When they looked inside, they found that there were cages in the lodges. Each cage held a different bird.

"These will make for fine hunting," Fisher said. "Let us set them free."

Gitchee Manitou placed Fisher high up in the sky among the stars.

Quickly Wolverine and Fisher chewed through the rawhide that bound the cages together and freed the birds. The birds all flew down through the hole in the sky. So there are many kinds of birds in the world today.

Wolverine and Fisher now began to make the hole in the skyland bigger. The warmth of the skyland began to fall through the hole and the land below began to grow warmer. The snow began to melt and the grass and plants beneath the snow began to turn green.

But the sky people came out when they saw what was happening. They ran toward Wolverine and Fisher, shouting loudly.

"Thieves," they shouted. "Stop taking our warm weather!"

Wolverine jumped back through the hole to escape, but Fisher kept making the hole bigger. He knew that if he didn't make it big enough, the sky people would quickly close the hole again and it would be winter again in the land below. He chewed the hole larger and larger. Finally, just when the sky people were very close, he stopped.

The hole was big enough for enough warm weather for half of the year to escape through, but it was not big enough for enough warm weather to last all the time. That is why the winter still comes back every year. Fisher knew that the sky people might try to close the hole in the sky. He had to take their attention away from it and so he taunted them.

"I am Fisher, the great hunter," he said. "You cannot catch me." Then he ran to the tallest tree in the skyland. All the sky people ran after him. Just as they were about to grab him, he leaped up into the tree and climbed to the highest branches, where no one could follow.

At first the sky people did not know what to do. Then they began to shoot arrows at him. But Fisher wasn't hurt, for he had a special power. There was only one place on his tail where an arrow could kill him. Finally, though, the sky people guessed where his magic was and shot at that place. An arrow struck the fatal spot. Fisher turned over on his back and began to fall.

But Fisher never struck the Earth. Gitchee Manitou took pity on him because he had kept his promise and done something to help all the people. Gitchee Manitou placed Fisher high up in the sky among the stars.

If you look up into the sky, you can still see him, even though some people call that pattern of stars The Big Dipper. Every year he crosses the sky. When the arrow strikes him, he rolls over onto his back in the winter sky. But when the winter is almost ended, he faithfully turns to his feet and starts out once more on his long journey to bring the warm weather back to the Earth.

Then they began to shoot arrows at him.

Seasons

His only friend was the North Wind.

✤

Seneca

Northeast Woodlands

Spring Defeats Winter

When the world was new, long ago, an old man was wandering around.

This old man had long, white hair and wherever he stepped the ground grew hard as stone. When he breathed the rivers stopped flowing and the ponds became solid. The birds and animals fled before him and plants dried up and died as the leaves shriveled and fell from the trees.

Finally, this old man found a place where he could set up his lodge. He made the walls of ice and covered it over with snow. He sat inside his lodge in front of a fire which gave off no heat, though a strange flickering light came from it. His only friend was the North Wind, who sat beside the fire with him and laughed as they spoke of things they did to make the world a cold, hard place. They sat and smoked their pipes through the long, white nights.

One morning, though, as the two dozed by their fire, they felt that something was wrong. The air was

The snowdrifts were growing smaller.

harder to breathe and when they looked outside, they saw strange things happening. The snowdrifts were growing smaller. Cracks were forming in the ice on the ponds.

"Henh!" said the North Wind. "I can stay no longer." He went out of the lodge and flew through the air toward the north, not stopping until he again reached a place where snow and ice were deep and there was no hint of warmth. But the old man did not stir. He knew his magic was strong. He had built his lodge to last.

Now, there came a knocking at his door. Someone was striking against the ice so hard that pieces were falling away from his blows. "Go away!" the old man shouted. "No one can enter my lodge."

Even as he said it, the door of the lodge broke and fell to the ground. A young man with a smile on his face stood there. Without a word he stepped into the lodge and sat on the other side of the fire from the old man. He held a green stick in his hand and with it he stirred the fire. As he stirred the fire it began to grow warm. The old man felt sweat begin to run down his face.

"Who are you?" said the old man. "Why have you broken my door? No one can come in here but my friend, North Wind. If you do not leave, I will freeze you with my breath." Then the old man tried to blow his chilly breath at the young

stranger, but only a thin mist came from his lips.

The young man laughed. "Old Man," he said, "let me stay here and warm myself by your fire."

The old man grew angry. "I am the one who makes the birds and the animals flee. Wherever I step the ground turns into flint. I make the snow and ice. I am mightier than you." As he spoke, though, the old man felt more sweat run off his brow, and the young man continued to smile.

"Listen," the stranger said, "I am young and strong. You cannot frighten me. Surely you know who I am. Do you not feel how warm my breath is? Wherever I breathe the plants grow and the flowers bloom. Where I step the grasses sprout and snow melts away. The birds and the animals come to me. See how long my hair is? Your hair is falling out now, Old Man. Wherever I travel I bring the sunshine and you cannot stay. Do you not know me, Old Man? Do you not hear my companion, the Fawn? She is the South Wind. She is blowing on your lodge. It is your time to leave."

The old man opened his mouth to speak, but no words came out. He grew smaller and smaller and the sweat poured from his brow as he melted away. Then he was gone. The walls of his lodge of ice and snow fell in. Where his cold fire had burned, white flowers now bloomed. Once again, the Young Man, Spring, had defeated the Old Man, Winter.

Wherever I breathe the plants grow and the flowers bloom.

Plants and Animals

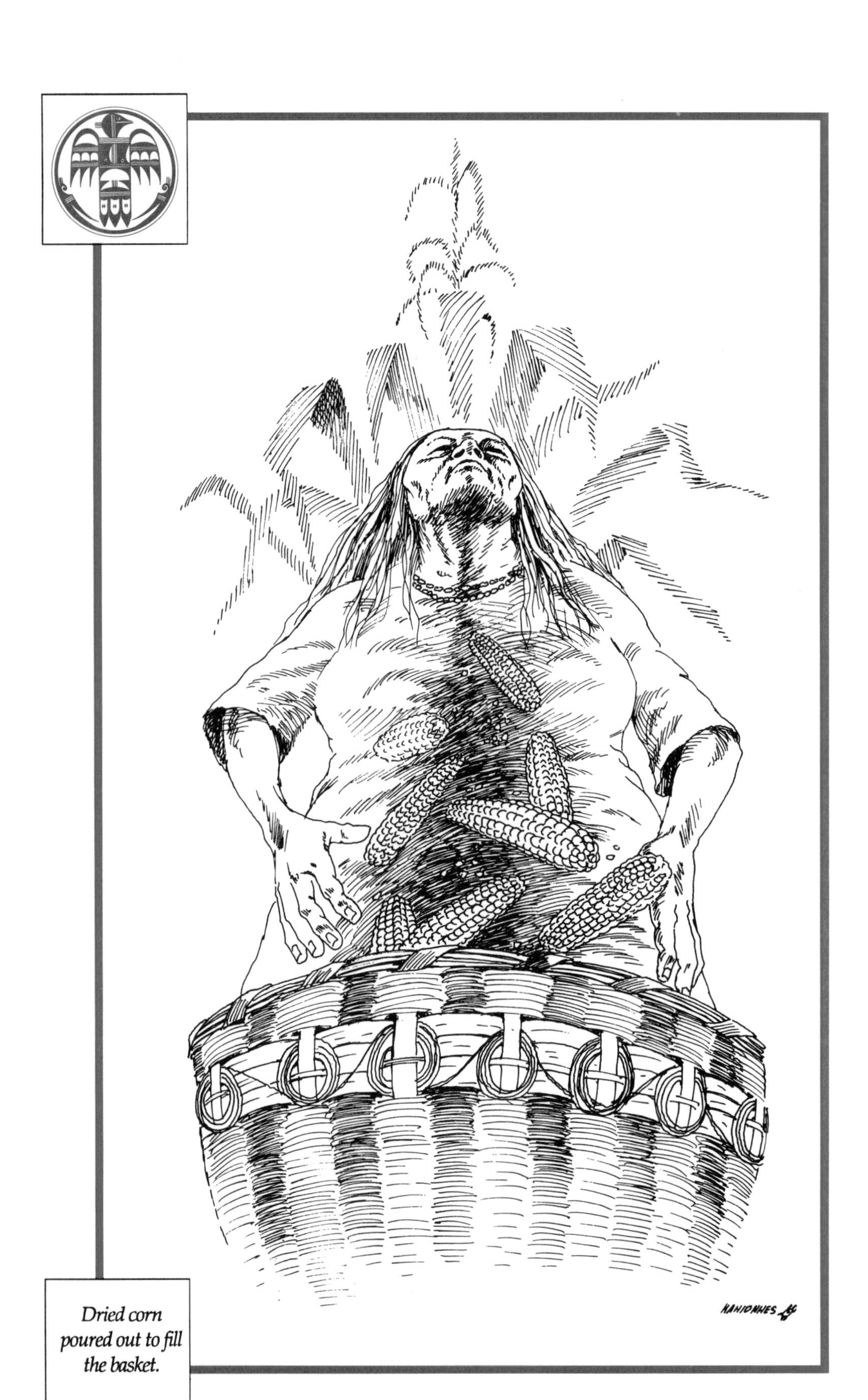

Dried corn poured out to fill the basket.

Cherokee

North Carolina

The Coming of Corn

Long ago, when the world was new, an old woman lived with her grandson in the shadow of the big mountain.

They lived happily together until the boy was seven years old. Then his Grandmother gave him his first bow and arrow. He went out to hunt for game and brought back a small bird.

"Ah," said the Grandmother, "You are going to be a great hunter. We must have a feast." She went out to the small storehouse behind their cabin. She came back with dried corn in her basket and made a fine-tasting soup with the small bird and the corn.

From that point on the boy hunted. Each day he brought back something and each day the Grandmother took some corn from the storage house to make soup. One day, though, the boy peeked into the storehouse. It was empty! But that evening, when he returned with game to cook, she went out again and brought back a basket filled with dry corn.

"This is strange," the boy said to himself. "I must find out what is happening."

The next day, when he brought back his game, he waited until his Grandmother had gone out for her basket of corn and followed her. He watched her go into the storehouse with the empty basket. He looked through a crack between the logs and saw a very strange thing. The storehouse was empty, but his grandmother was leaning over the basket. She rubbed her hand along the side of her body, and dried corn poured out to fill the basket. Now the boy grew afraid. Perhaps she was a witch! He crept back to the house to wait. When his Grandmother returned, though, she saw the look on his face.

"Grandson," she said, "you followed me to the shed and saw what I did there."

"Yes, Grandmother," the boy answered.

The old woman shook her head sadly. "Grandson," she said, "then I must get ready to leave you. Now that you know my secret I can no longer live with you as I did before. Before the sun rises tomorrow I shall be dead. You must do as I tell you, and you will be able to feed yourself and the people when I have gone."

The old woman looked very weary and the boy started to move toward her, but she motioned him away. "You

He watched her go into the storehouse with the empty basket.

cannot help now, Grandson. Simply do as I tell you. When I have died, clear away a patch of ground on the south side of our lodge, that place where the sun shines longest and brightest. The earth there must be made completely bare. Drag my body over that ground seven times and then bury me in that earth. Keep the ground clear. If you do as I say, you shall see me again and you will be able to feed the people." Then the old woman grew silent and closed her eyes. Before the morning came, she was dead.

Her grandson did as he was told. He cleared away the space at the south side of the cabin. It was hard work, for there were trees and tangled vines, but at last the earth was bare. He dragged his Grandmother's body, and wherever a drop of her blood fell a small plant grew up. He kept the ground clear around the small plants, and as they grew taller it seemed he could hear his Grandmother's voice whispering in the leaves. Time passed and the plants grew very tall, as tall as a person, and the long tassels at the top of each plant reminded the boy of his grandmother's long hair. At last, ears of corn formed on each plant and his Grandmother's promise had come true. Now, though she had gone from the Earth as she had once been, she would be with the people forever as the corn plant, to feed them.

They were in the grove of maple trees near the village.

Anishinabe

Great Lakes Region

Manabozho and the Maple Trees

A long time ago, when the world was new, Gitchee Manitou made things so that life was very easy for the people.

There was plenty of game and the weather was always good and the maple trees were filled with thick sweet syrup. Whenever anyone wanted to get maple syrup from the trees, all they had to do was break off a twig and collect it as it dripped out.

One day, Manabozho went walking around. "I think I'll go see how my friends the Anishinabe are doing," he said. So he went to a village of Indian people. But there was no one around. So Manabozho looked for the people. They were not fishing in the streams or the lake. They were not working in the fields hoeing their crops. They were not gathering berries. Finally he found them. They were in the grove of maple trees near the village. They were all just lying on their backs with their mouths open, letting the maple syrup drip into their mouths.

ANISHINABE
(OJIBWAY or CHIPPEWA)
Menominee

"This will not do," Manabozho said. "My people are all going to be fat and lazy if they keep on living this way."

So Manabozho went down to the river. He took with him a big basket he had made of birch bark. With this basket he brought back many buckets of water. He went to the top of the maple trees and poured the water in so that it thinned out the syrup. Now thick maple syrup no longer dripped out of the broken twigs. Now what came out was thin and watery and just barely sweet to the taste.

"This is how it will be from now on," Manabozho said. "No longer will syrup drip from the maple trees. Now there will be only this watery sap. When people want to make maple syrup they will have to gather many buckets full of the sap in a birch bark basket like mine. They will have to gather wood and make fires so they can heat stones to drop into the baskets. They will have to boil the water with the heated stones for a long time to make even a little maple syrup. Then my people will no longer grow fat and lazy. Then they will appreciate this maple syrup Gitchee Manitou made available to them. Not only that, this sap will drip only from the trees at a certain time of the year. Then it will not keep people from hunting and fishing and gathering and hoeing in the fields. This is how it is going to be," Manabozho said.

And that is how it is to this day.

"This is how it is going to be."

Kokopilau, the Hump-Backed Flute Player

After the Hopi people had come out of the sipapu into the Fourth World, they were told by Masaw, the ruler of this world, that they must migrate to the four directions before they could come to the place where they would finally settle.

So their travels began.

There are many stories of these migrations. More than one of them tells of Kokopilau, an insect person who accompanied them. Carvings which depict Kokopilau can be found in rocks from South America to Canada, and the Hopi people say this is proof of how far they traveled. You can see Kokopilau's long antennae branching out from his head in many of those rock drawings, for Kokopilau was a locust or a grasshopper. He was also a flute player and a trickster of sorts, as the following story shows.

Near the start of their migrations, the Hopi people climbed to the top of a mountain.

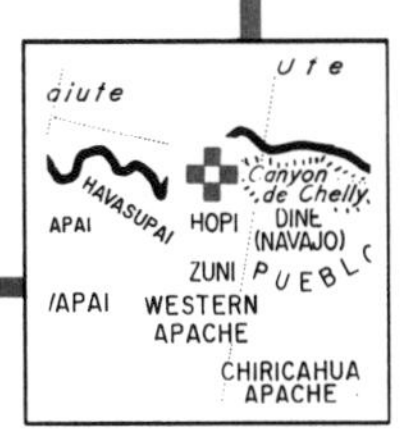

On top of that mountain was a great Eagle.

"I am the one who guards this place," said the Eagle. "I have lived here since this Fourth World was created. Anyone who would pass into this land must pass my test."

Then Kokopilau stepped forward. "We wish to live in this land," he said. "I am ready to be tested."

"I am the one who guards this place."

At that the Eagle drew forth an arrow. "You must be able to do as I do," he said. Then the Eagle pierced himself with the arrow and drew it with great effort out the other side without hurting himself.

"That is easy," said Kokopilau, taking the arrow and passing it quickly under his wing covers so that it seemed the arrow had pierced him and come out the other side.

"I see that you have great power, indeed," said the Eagle. "You have my permission to lead your people into this new land. You may also use my feathers for your prayer sticks whenever you wish to speak with the Creator. As I am the one who flies the highest and closest to the Sun, your prayers will be taken up to the Creator quickly." So it was that ever since then, the Eagle's feathers have been placed on the *pahos*, or prayer sticks, of the Hopi people.

Then Kokopilau led the people into the new land. As he played his flute, the land and the winds became warm. In the hump on his back he carried seeds of useful plants. Thus the corn and beans and squash and flowers began to grow as the people traveled with the Hump-backed Flute Player across the beautiful new Fourth World in those early days.

"Isn't there some way you could take me along?"

Dakota
[Sioux]

Midwest

How Turtle Flew South for the Winter

It was the time of year when the leaves start to fall from the aspens.

Turtle was walking around when he saw many birds gathering together in the trees. They were making a lot of noise and Turtle was curious. "Hey," Turtle said, "What is happening?"

"Don't you know?" the birds said. "We're getting ready to fly to the south for the winter."

"Why are you going to do that?" Turtle said.

"Don't you know anything?" the birds said. "Soon it's going to be very cold here and the snow will fall. There won't be much food to eat. Down south it will be warm. Summer lives there all of the time and there's plenty of food."

As soon as they mentioned the food, Turtle became even more interested. "Can I come with you?" he said.

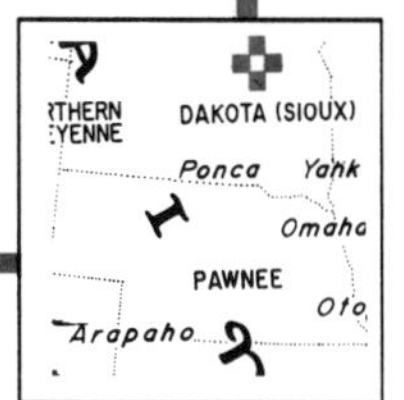

"You have to fly to go south," said the birds. "You are a turtle and you can't fly."

But Turtle would not give up. "Isn't there some way you could take me along?" He begged and pleaded. Finally the birds agreed just to get him to stop asking.

"Look here," the birds said, "can you hold onto a stick hard with your mouth?"

"That's no problem at all," Turtle said. "Once I grab onto something no one can make me let go until I am ready."

"Good," said the birds. "Then you hold on hard to this stick. These two birds here will each grab one end of it in their claws. That way they can carry you along. But remember, you have to keep your mouth shut!"

"That's easy," said Turtle. "Now let's go south where Summer keeps all that food." Turtle grabbed onto the middle of the stick and two big birds came and grabbed each end. They flapped their wings hard and lifted Turtle off the ground. Soon they were high in the sky and headed toward the south.

Turtle had never been so high off the ground before, but he liked it. He could look down and see how small everything looked. But before they had gone too far, he began to wonder where they were. He wondered what the lake was

Turtle had never been so high off the ground before, but he liked it.

down below him and what those hills were. He wondered how far they had come and how far they would have to go to get to the south where Summer lived. He wanted to ask the two birds who were carrying him, but he couldn't talk with his mouth closed.

Turtle rolled his eyes. But the two birds just kept on flying. Then Turtle tried waving his legs at them, but they acted as if they didn't even notice. Now Turtle was getting upset. If they were going to take him south, then the least they could do was tell him where they were now! "Mmmph," Turtle said, trying to get their attention. It didn't work. Finally Turtle lost his temper.

"Why don't you listen to . . . " but that was all he said, for as soon as he opened his mouth to speak, he had to let go of the stick and he started to fall. Down and down he fell, a long, long way. He was so frightened that he pulled his legs and his head in to protect himself! When he hit the ground he hit so hard that his shell cracked. He was lucky that he hadn't been killed, but he ached all over. He ached so much that he crawled into a nearby pond, swam down to the bottom and dug into the mud to get as far away from the sky as he possibly could. Then he fell asleep and he slept all through the winter and didn't wake up until the spring.

So it is that today only the birds fly south to the land where summer lives while turtles, who all have cracked shells now, sleep through the winter.

She wove it together tight and strong, and it was a fine game bag.

Abenaki

Northeast Woodlands

Gluscabi and the Game Animals

Long ago Gluscabi decided he would do some hunting.

He took his bow and arrows and went into the woods.

But all the animals said to each other, "Ah-hah, here comes Gluscabi. He is hunting us. Let us hide from him."

So they hid and Gluscabi could not find them. He was not pleased. He went home to the little lodge near the big water where he lived with Grandmother Woodchuck.

"Grandmother," he said, "Make a game bag for me."

So Grandmother Woodchuck took caribou hair and made him a game bag. She wove it together tight and strong, and it was a fine game bag. But when she gave it to Gluscabi, he looked at it and then threw it down.

"This is not good enough," he said.

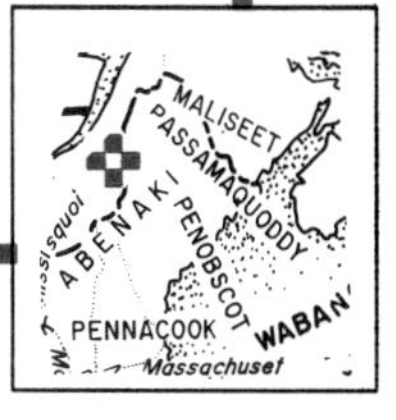

No matter how much you put into it, there would still be room for more.

So then Grandmother Woodchuck took deer hair. She wove a larger and finer game bag and gave it to him. But Gluscabi looked at it and threw it down.

"This is not good enough, Grandmother," he said.

Now Grandmother Woodchuck took moose hair and wove him a very fine game bag indeed. It was large and strong, and she took porcupine quills which she flattened with her teeth, and she wove a design into the game bag to make it even more attractive. But Gluscabi looked at this game bag, too, and threw it down.

"Grandmother," he said. "This is not good enough."

"Eh, Gluscabi," said Grandmother Woodchuck, "how can I please you? What kind of game bag do you want?"

Then Gluscabi smiled. "Ah, Grandmother," he said, "make one out of woodchuck hair."

So Grandmother Woodchuck pulled all of the hair from her belly. To this day you will see that all woodchucks still have no hair there. Then she wove it into a game bag. Now this game bag was magical. No matter how much you put into it, there would still be room for more. And Gluscabi took this game bag and smiled.

"Oleohneh, Grandmother," he said. "I thank you."

Now Gluscabi went back into the woods and walked until he came to a large clearing. Then he called out as loudly as he could, "All you animals, listen to me. A terrible thing is going to happen. The sun is going to go out. The world is going to end and everything is going to be destroyed."

When the animals heard that, they became frightened. They came to the clearing where Gluscabi stood with his magic game bag. "Gluscabi," they said, "What can we do? The world is going to be destroyed. How can we survive?"

Gluscabi smiled. "My friends," he said, "just climb into my game bag. Then you will be safe in there when the world is destroyed."

So all of the animals went into his game bag. The rabbits and the squirrels went in, and the game bag stretched to hold them. The raccoons and the foxes went in, and the game bag stretched larger still. The deer went in and the caribou went in. The bears went in and the moose went in, and the game bag stretched to hold them all. Soon all the animals in the world were in Gluscabi's game bag. Then Gluscabi tied the top of the game bag, laughed, slung it over his shoulder and went home.

"Grandmother," he said, "now we no longer have to go out and walk around looking for food. Whenever we want anything to eat we can just reach into my game bag."

So all of the animals went into his game bag.

Grandmother Woodchuck opened Gluscabi's game bag and looked inside. There were all of the animals in the world.

"Oh, Gluscabi," she said, "why must you always do things this way? You cannot keep all of the game animals in a bag. They will sicken and die. There will be none left for our children and our children's children. It is also right that it should be difficult to hunt them. Then you will grow stronger trying to find them. And the animals will also grow stronger and wiser trying to avoid being caught. Then things will be in the right balance."

"Kaamoji, Grandmother," said Gluscabi, "That is so." So he picked up his game bag and went back to the clearing. He opened it up. "All you animals," he called, "you can come out now. Everything is all right. The world was destroyed, but I put it back together again."

Then all of the animals came out of the magic game bag. They went back into the woods, and they are still there today because Gluscabi heard what his Grandmother Woodchuck had to say.

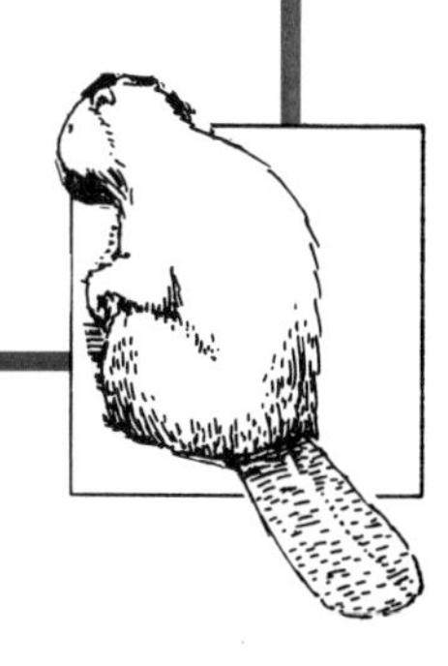

Awi Usdi, Little Deer, was their leader.

Cherokee

North Carolina

Awi Usdi, the Little Deer

Back when the world was young, the humans and the animal people could speak to each other.

At first they lived in peace. The humans hunted the animals only when they needed food or skins to make clothing. Then the humans discovered the bow and arrow. With this new weapon they could kill many animals quickly and with great ease. They began to kill animals when they did not need them for food or clothing. It seemed as if all the animals in the world would soon be exterminated. So the various animals met in council.

When the bears came together and talked about what the humans were doing, they decided they would have to fight back.

"How can we do that?" said one of the bear warriors. "The humans will shoot us with their arrows before we come close to them." Old Bear, their chief, agreed. "That is true. We must learn how to use the same weapons they use."

Then the bears made a very strong bow and fashioned arrows for it. But whenever they tried to use the bow, their long claws got in the way.

"I will cut off my claws," said one of the bear warriors. He did so and then he was able to use the bow and arrow. His aim was good and he hit the mark every time.

"That is good," said Old Bear. "Now can you climb this tree?" The bear without claws tried to climb the tree, but he failed. Old Bear shook his head. "This will not do. Without our claws we cannot climb trees. Without our claws we will not be able to hunt or dig for food. We must give up this idea of using the same weapons the humans use."

So the bears gave up their idea of fighting back against the humans with weapons.

One by one each of the animal groups met. One by one they came to no conclusion. It seemed there was no way to fight back. But the last group to meet was the deer.

Awi Usdi, Little Deer, was their leader. When all were gathered together, he spoke.

"I see what we must do," he said. "We cannot stop the humans from hunting animals. That is the way it was meant to be. However, the humans are not doing things in

One by one each of the animal groups met.

the right way. If they do not respect us and hunt us only when there is real need, they may kill us all. I shall go now and tell the hunters what they must do. Whenever they wish to kill a deer, they must prepare in a ceremonial way. They must ask me for permission to kill one of us. Then, after they kill a deer, they must show respect to its spirit and ask for pardon. If the hunters do not do this, then I shall track them down. With my magic I will make their limbs crippled. Then they will no longer be able to walk or shoot a bow and arrow."

Then Awi Usdi, Little Deer, did as he said. He went at night and whispered into the ears of the hunters, telling them what they must do. The next morning, when they awoke, some of the hunters thought they had been dreaming and they were not sure that the dream was a true one.

Others, though, realized that Little Deer, Awi Usdi, had truly spoken to them. They tried to do as he told them. They hunted for the deer and other animals only when they needed food and clothing. They remembered to prepare in a ceremonial way, to ask permission before killing an animal and to ask pardon when an animal was killed.

Some of the hunters, though, paid no attention. They continued to kill animals for no reason. But Awi Usdi, Little Deer, came to them and, using his magic, crippled them with rheumatism. Before long, all of the hunters began to treat the animals with respect and to follow Little Deer's teachings.

So it is that the animals have survived to this day.

Because of Awi Usdi, Little Deer, the Indian people show respect. To this day, even though the animals and people no longer can speak to each other as in the old days, the people still show respect and give thanks to the animals they must hunt.

Because of Awi Usdi, Little Deer, the Indian people show respect.

Life, Death, Spirit

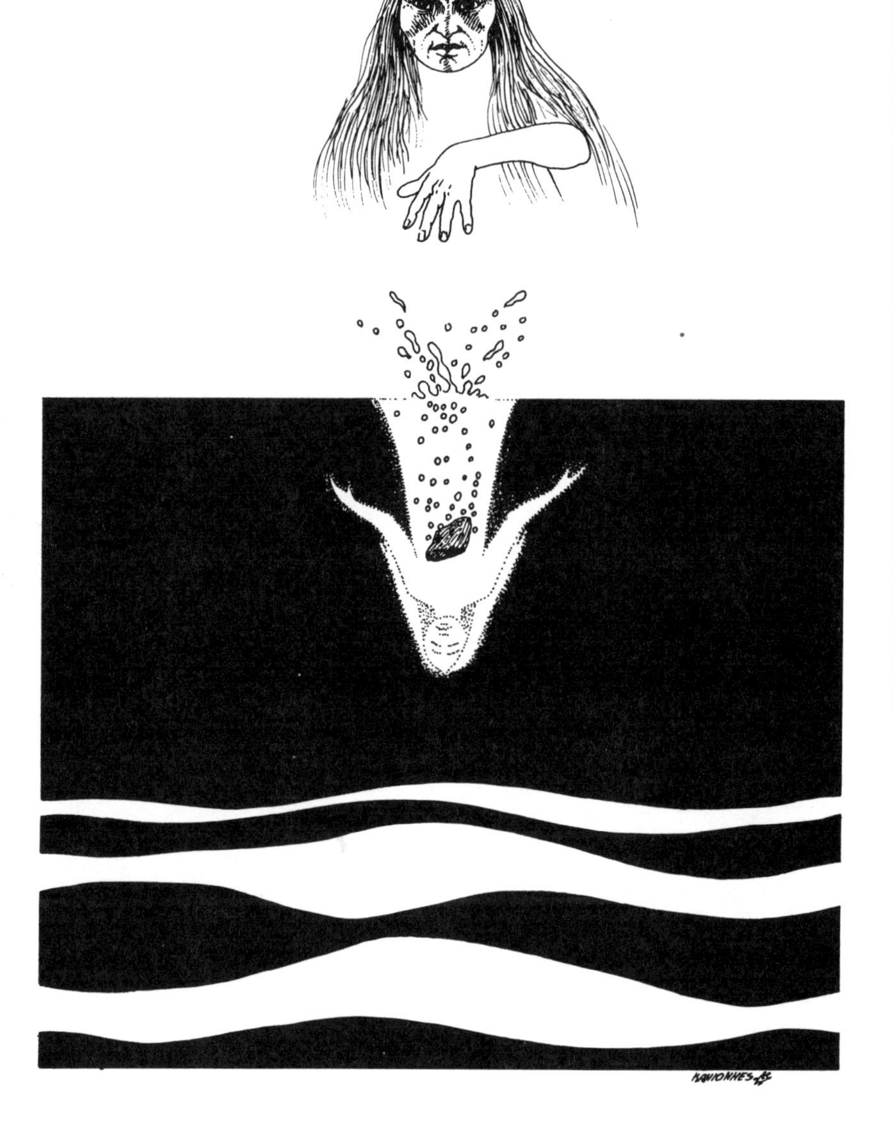

I will throw this stone into the water instead.

The Origin of Death

When the world was new, Old Man and Old Woman were walking around.

"Let us decide how things will be," Old Man said.

"That is good," said Old Woman. "How shall we do it?"

"Well," Old Man said, "since it was my idea I think I should have the first say in everything."

"That is good," said Old Woman, "just as long as I have the last say."

So they walked around and looked at things. Then Old Man spoke. "I have been thinking about hunting," he said. "The men will be the hunters. Anytime they want to shoot an animal they will call it and it will come to them."

"I agree men should be the hunters," Old Woman said. "But if the animals come when they are called, life will

be too easy for the people. The animals should run away when they see the people. Then it will be hard for the men to kill them. That way people will be smarter and stronger."

"You have the last say," Old Man agreed. Then they walked around some more.

After a while, Old Man spoke again. "I have been thinking about what people will look like," he said. "They will have eyes on one side of their face and their mouth on the other. Their mouths will go straight up and down. They will have ten fingers on each hand."

"I agree that people should have their eyes and their mouth on their faces," Old Woman said. "But their eyes will be at the top of their face and their mouth at the bottom and they will be set across. I agree they should have fingers on their hands, but ten on each hand will make them clumsy. They will have five fingers on each hand."

"You have the last say," Old Man agreed.

Now they were walking by the river. "Let us decide about life and death," Old Man said. "I will do it this way. I will throw this buffalo chip into the river. If it floats, when people die they will come back to life after four days and then live forever."

"You have the last say," Old Man agreed.

Old Man threw the buffalo chip into the water. It bobbed up and floated. "I agree we should decide it this way," Old Woman said. "But I do not think it should be done with a buffalo chip. I will throw this stone into the water instead. If it floats, the people will die for four days and then come back to life and live forever. If it sinks, the people will not come back to life after they die."

Old Woman threw the stone into the water. It sank immediately.

"That is the way it should be," Old Woman said. "If people lived forever, the Earth would be too crowded. There would not be enough food. This way people will feel sorry for each other. There will be sympathy in the world."

Old Man said nothing.

Some time passed. Old Woman had a child. She and Old Man loved the child very much and they were happy. One day, though, the child became sick and died. Then Old Woman went to Old Man.

"Let us have our say again about death," she said.

But Old Man shook his head. "No," he said, "you had the last say."

Unity of Earth

In her hands she carried the bundle and a bunch of sacred sage.

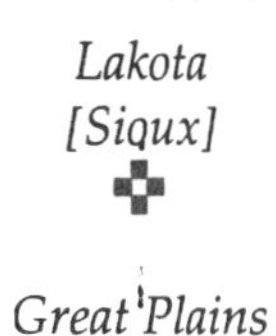

The White Buffalo Calf Woman and the Sacred Pipe

It was a time when there was little food left in the camp and the people were hungry.

Two young men were sent out to scout for game. They went on foot, for this was a time long before the horses, the great Spirit Dogs, were given to the people. The two young men hunted a long time but had no luck. Finally, they climbed to the top of a hill and looked to the west.

"What is that?" said one of the young men.

"I cannot tell, but it is coming toward us," said the other.

And so it was. At first they thought that it was an animal, but as the shape drew closer they saw it was a woman. She was dressed in white buffalo skin and carried something in her hands. She walked so lightly that it seemed as if she was not walking at all, but floating with her feet barely touching the Earth.

Then the first young man realized that she must be a Holy Person and his mind filled with good thoughts. But the second young man did not see her that way. He saw her only as a beautiful young woman and his mind filled with bad thoughts. She was now very close and he reached out to grab her. As soon as he did so, though, there was a sound of lightning and the young man was covered by a cloud. When it cleared away there was nothing left of the second young man but a skeleton.

Then the White Buffalo Calf Woman spoke. "Go to your people," she said, holding up the bundle in her hands so that the first young man could see it. "Tell your people that it is a good thing I am bringing. I am bringing a holy thing to your nation, a message from the Buffalo People. Put up a medicine lodge for me and make it ready. I will come there after four days have passed."

The first young man did as he was told. He went back to his people and gave them the message. Then the crier went through the camp and told all the people that something sacred was coming and that all things should be made ready. They built the medicine lodge and made an earth altar which faced the west.

Four days passed and then the people saw something coming toward them. When it came closer, they saw it was the White Buffalo Calf Woman. In her hands

Put up a medicine lodge for me and make it ready.

she carried the bundle and a bunch of sacred sage. The people welcomed her into the medicine lodge and gave her the seat of honor. Then she unwrapped the bundle to show them what was inside. It was the Sacred Pipe. As she held it out to them she told them what it meant.

"The bowl of the Pipe," she said, "is made of the red stone. It represents the flesh and blood of the Buffalo People and all other Peoples. The wooden stem of the Pipe represents all the trees and plants, all the things green and growing on this Earth. The smoke that passes through the Pipe represents the sacred wind, the breath that carries prayers up to Wakan Tanka, the Creator."

When she finished showing them the Pipe, she told the people how to hold it and how to offer it to Earth and Sky and the Four Sacred Directions. She told them many things to remember.

"The Sacred Pipe," said the White Buffalo Calf Woman, "will show you the Good Red Road. Follow it and it will take you in the right direction. Now," she said, "I am going to leave, but you will see me again."

Then she began to walk toward the setting sun. The people watched her as she went, and they saw her stop and roll once on the Earth. When she stood up she was a black buffalo. Then she went farther and rolled again on the Earth. This time when she stood up she was a brown buffalo. She went farther and rolled a third time and stood up. Now the people saw that she was a red buffalo. Again she walked farther and for a fourth and final time she rolled upon the Earth. This time she became a white buffalo calf and continued to walk until she disappeared over the horizon.

As soon as the White Buffalo Calf Woman was gone, herds of buffalo were seen all around the camp. The people were able to hunt them and they gave thanks with the Sacred Pipe for the blessings they had been given. As long as they followed the Good Red Road of the Sacred Pipe and remembered, as the White Buffalo Calf Woman taught them, that all things were as connected as parts of the Pipe, they lived happily and well.

Then she began to walk toward the setting sun.

Glossary and Pronunciation Key

The following rules are used for the phonetic description of how each word is pronounced:

1. A line appears over long vowels. Short vowels are unmarked. For instance, "date" would appear as dāt, while "bat" would appear as bat.
2. An accent mark (´) shows which syllable in each word or name is the one emphasized.
3. Syllables are broken with a hyphen (-).
4. Syllables are spelled out as they are pronounced. For instance, "Cherokee" appears as "chair-oh-key."

Where appropriate, the culture from which each word or name comes is given in brackets [ ], followed by the meaning of that word or name, or an explanation of its significance as it appears in the text.

Abenaki (Ab´-er-na-kee or Ab´-eh-na-kee). People living at the sunrise, "People of the Dawn." A northeastern Algonquian group.
Adlivun (ahd-lih´-vun). [Inuit] land under the sea.
adobe (ah-dō´-bey). [Spanish, from Arabic atobe] sun dried bricks.
Aja (Ah´-ha). [Inuit] name of Sedna's father in *Sedna, the Woman Under the Sea.*
Algonquian (Al-gon´-kee-en). Large diverse grouping of native peoples related by a common linguistic root. Algonquian Indians live in the Atlantic coastal regions from what we now call the Maritime Provinces of Canada, to the southeastern United States, west to the central provinces and down through the central states into Wyoming and Montana.
Angakok (An-gah-kok). [Inuit] a shaman. *See* shaman.
Anishinabe (Ah-nish-ih-nah´-bey). Correct name of people known as Ojibway or Chippewa, means the "People."
Apache (Ah-patch´-ē). [Zuni Pueblo *ahpachu,* meaning the "Enemy"] word used commonly today to refer to the people who call themselves *Tineh* (tih-ney)—the "People."
Awi Usdi (Ah´-wee Oos´-dee). [Cherokee] little deer.
Begochiddy (Bey´-go-chid-dee). [Navajo] Creator god.

Blackfeet. People of the western plains and mountains straddling the Montana–Alberta border who call themselves *siksika* (sik-sih´-ka), which means "Black Foot," referring to their black-dyed moccasins.

Cañon de Chelly (Kan-yun´ de Shāy). [Spanish] canyon in the Four Corners area of the southwestern United States with many ancient ruins.

Cayuga (Kah´-yū-gah). [Iroquois] one of the six nations of the Iroquois confederacy. "People of the Swampy Land."

Cherokee (Chair-oh-kēy´). Corruption of a Lenni Lenape [Delaware] Indian name (*Talligewi* or *Tsa la gi*) for this very large southeastern tribe who called themselves *Ani Yunwiya* (Ah-nēē Yūhn-wī-yah)—"Real People." One of the so-called (by whites) "Five Civilized Tribes."

Cheyenne (Shy´-ann). Corruption of Lakota word *shyela*, "Those Who Speak a Strange Tongue." Refers to a people of the northern Great Plains. Their own name for themselves is *Dzitsista* (Gee-tsi-stah), meaning "Our People."

Chickasaw (Chick´-ah-saw). A people of the southeast, northern Alabama, northern Mississippi—Meaning of name appears to be lost; probably means the "People." One of so-called "Five Civilized Tribes."

Chippewa (Chip´-ah-wah). *See* Anishinabe.

Choctaw (Chock´-taw). A people of Mississippi and Alabama. One of so-called "Five Civilized Tribes."

Clan Mother. Elder woman regarded as the head of a particular clan. Among matrilineal people such as the Iroquois, a Clan Mother has great power and is a major political force.

Colville (Kol´-vill). A native people of the Salish language family found in eastern Washington State.

Comanche (Ko-man´-che). Corruption of Ute word, *komon´teia*, "One Who Wants to Always Fight Me." A people of the southern Great Plains.

Creek (Krēēk). Name used for the people who call themselves *Muskogee* (Mus-ko-gee), probably because white traders found their villages along streams from the Atlantic coast of Georgia through central Alabama. One of the so-called "Five Civilized Tribes."

Crow (Krō). Name usually applied to the native people of the northern Great Plains who call themselves *Absaroke* (Ahb-sah-rokuh), which means "Bird People," but could also mean "Crow."

Dakota (Dah-ko´-tah), "Sioux." One of the seven main "council fires" of the Sioux people. *Dakota* is in the Santee Sioux dialect, means "Allies," refers to the Sioux of eastern plains, Minnesota. Sioux called themselves *Ocheti shakowin* (Oh-che-ti shah-kō-win), the "Seven Council Fires."

Dine (Dih-nēy´), "Navajo." Means the "People."

Eskimo (Es´-kih-mō). Cree word meaning "Fish Eaters," applied to the people who call themselves *Inuit*—the "People."

Gitchee Manitou (Gih-chēē´ Man´-ē-too). [Anishinabe] the Great Spirit.

Glooskap (Gloo´-skap). Trickster figure of northern Wabanaki peoples such as the Micmac of Nova Scotia.

Gluscabi (Gloos´-kah-bē). Trickster hero of southern and midwestern Wabanaki such as the Penobscot of Maine. Gluscabi means "Teller of Stories."

Great League "Iroquois." The alliance of peace forged among the formerly warring five nations of the Iroquois about 500 years or more ago by the Peacemakers and Hiawatha.

hageota (hah-gey´-oh-da). [Iroquois] a storyteller.

Haida (hi´-dah). Pacific northwest Indian group of Queen Charlotte Islands, British Columbia, and the southern end of Prince of Wales Island, Alaska. Called Kaigani in Alaska. Known for their beautiful carvings, paintings and totem poles.

Haudenausaunee (Ho-dē-nō-show´-nē). [Iroquois] Iroquois name for themselves which means "People of the Longhouse."

Ha-wen-neyu (Hah-wen-ney´-oo). [Iroquois] The Creator.

Henh (hẽy [nasalized]). [Iroquois] expression used by storyteller to elicit response.

Hero Twins. Hopi, Navajo and Pueblo traditional stories have these two playful and powerful children as heroes who kill monsters.

Hiawatha (Hi-ah-wah´-tha). [Iroquois] corruption of *Ayontwatha*, which means "He Who Combs," the Mohawk who helped found the Great League.

hogan (ho´-gun). [Navajo] traditional dwelling made of logs and earth used by the Navajo.

Hopi (Ho´-pēē). Contraction of *Hopitu*, the "Peaceful Ones," the names used for themselves by a town-dwelling native people of northeastern Arizona.

Inuit (In´-you-it), "Eskimo." The "People," name used for themselves by the native peoples of the farthest Arctic regions, Iceland, Arctic Asia. Not regarded by themselves or Indians as American Indian.

Inung (In-ung´). Inuit name.

Iroquois (Ear´-oh-kwah). Corruption of an Algonquian word *Ireohkwa*, meaning "Real Snakes." Applied commonly to the Six Nations, the Haudenausaunee.

Ji-hi-ya (gēē´-hi-yah). [Iroquois] vocables used in song.

kaamoji (kaa-mō´-gee). [Abenaki] an exclamation.

kachina (kah-chee´-nah). [Hopi] sacred dancers or spirit people who bring rain, equated with ancestors and clouds.

Kahionhes (Gah-hē-yōn-heys). [Mohawk (Iroquois)] name meaning "Long River."

Kalispel (Kahl-ih-spell´). A native people of northern Idaho. Name probably refers to the camas, an edible plant found there.

Kan-ya-ti-yo (Gah-nya-di´-yō). [Iroquois (Seneca)] name of a lake, Lake Ontario, meaning "Beautiful Lake."

Kiowa (Ki´-yō-wah). Native people of southern Great Plains (southwest Oklahoma). Name means "Principal People."

kiva (kē´-vah). [Hopi] a chamber, usually underground, used for ceremonies.

ki yo wah ji neh, yo ho hey ho. [Seneca] vocables used in a canoe song

Klickitat (Klick´-ih-taht). A people found at the confluence of Klickitat and Columbia Rivers in the northwestern United States. Name means "Beyond," referring to the fact they are beyond the Cascade Mountains.

Kokopilau (Kō-kō-pēē´-le). [Hopi] hump-backed flute player kachina.

Koluscap (Koh-lūs´-kap). [Wabanaki] variation of Glooscap, Gluscabi.

Kwakiutl (Kwah-kē´-yūt-ul). A people of the Pacific northwest, British Columbia coast.

Lakota (Lah-ko´-tah). *See* Dakota. "Sioux" native people of northern plains, Nebraska, Dakotas.

longhouse. Large traditional dwelling of Iroquois people. Framework of saplings covered with elm bark with central fires and, to each side, compartments for families.

Loo-Wit (Lū´-wit). [Nisqually] Indian name for Mount Saint Helens.

Lummi (Lum´-mē). a Salish language-speaking people of Pacific Northwest.

Maliseet (Mahl-ih-sēēt´). [Abenaki] An Abenaki people of New Brunswick.

Manabozho (Man-ah-bō´-zo). [Algonquian] Algonquian trickster hero, "Old Man."

Masaw (Mah-saw). [Hopi] spirit of death.

medicine lodge. Small lodge used for curing ceremonies among northeastern native peoples.

medicine man. General term used to refer to "Indian doctors" who effect cures with a blend of psychiatry and sound herbal remedies, as well as by use of spiritual means. Each Indian nation has its own word for this person.

Mesquakie (Mes-kwah´-kēē). A native people of Iowa miscalled "Sac and Fox." "Red Earth People."

Micmac (Mihk´-mack). [Abenaki] A native people of Maritime Provinces. Name means "Our Allies."

Mohawk (Mō´-hawk). Abenaki word *maquak,* used to refer to the Iroquois who lived in area of Mohawk Valley in New York State and called themselves *Ganeagaono* (Flint People). Name means "Cowards."

Multnomah (Mult-nō´-mah). Chinookan language-speaking people of the Pacific Northwest in Oregon next to the Columbia River.

Muskogee (Mus-kō´-jēē). *See* Creek.

Naho (nah´-hō). [Iroquois] "I have spoken."

Navajo (Nah´-vah-hō). *See* Dine.

Nez Percé (Nehz Purse). A native people of northwest Idaho, western Washington. Name means "Pierced Nose" in French, misunderstanding of word for themselves *Choo-pin-it-pa-loo* ("People of the Mountain") for *Chopunnish* ("Pierced Noses").

Nisqually (Nis-kwal-lēē´). Salish language-speaking people of Pacific Northwest near Puget Sound.

nudatlogit (nū-daht-lō´-giht). [Abenaki (Penobscot)] "storyteller."

Odzihozo (Ōh-jēē´-hō-zō). [Western Abenaki] transformer hero.

Name means "He Gathers Himself," or the "Man Who Made Himself."
Ojibway (Oh-jib´-wah). *See* Anishinabe.
oleohneh (oh-lēē-oh´-ney). [Abenaki] "Thank you."
Oneida (Oh-ny´-dah). [Iroquois] one of the Six Nations. Their name for themselves was *Onayatakono,* "People of the Standing Stone."
Onondaga (On-un-dah´-gah). [Iroquois] the centralmost of the Six Nations, the "Fire-keepers." Name for themselves is *Onundagaono,* "People on the Hills."
Oot-kwah-tah (Ood-gwah´-dah). [Iroquois] the Pleiades, the "Seven Dancers."
Opis (Oh´-pihs). [Yurok] place name on California coast.
pahos (pah´-hōs). [Hopi] prayer feathers.
Pai (Pī). A Yuman people of the Grand Canyon region.
Papago (pah´-pah-gō). Southwest Indian group of southern Arizona, nomadic horticulturalists, prolific basket weavers. Two-thirds of the roughly 13,500 Papagos today live on reservations located mostly in Pima County, Arizona, with some living in Sonora State, Mexico.
Passamaquoddy (Pass-ah-mah-kwah´-dē). People of eastern Maine. Means "At the Plenty of Pollack Place."
Pawnee (Paw-nēē´). A people of the northern Great Plains, Nebraska. Name may mean "Horn" or "Hunters." They call themselves *Chahiksichohiks*—"Men of Men."
Pennacook (Pen´-ah-kuhk). Abenaki people of New Hampshire. Means "Down Hill."
Penobscot (Pen-ahb´-skot). Abenaki people of central Maine. Means the "Rocky Place."
Pimas (Pē´-ma). A native people of southern Arizona who call themselves *O-o-dam,* the "People." *Pima* means "no" in the language of the nearby Nevome Indians.
potlatch (pot´-latch). Chinook trade language word from Nootka word, *patshall,* meaning "gift." A "giving-away" ceremony practiced among certain Pacific Northwest Salish native peoples.
Pueblo (Pweb´-lō). Spanish for town, refers to a number of "town-dwelling" native peoples along the Rio Grande in New Mexico who live in large adobe buildings like apartment complexes.
Sedna (Sed´-nah). [Inuit] name of woman who becomes the "Goddess of the World Below the Sea."
Seminole (Sem´-ih-nōl). A branch of the lower Creek peoples who united with the Yuchi, Oconee and other peoples in Florida to form a mixed nation in the 18th century. The name means "Runaways."
Seneca (Sen´-eh-ka). Corruption of an Algonquian word *O-sin-in-ka,* meaning "People of the Stone." Refers to the westernmost of the Six Nations, "Keepers of the Western Door." The Iroquois who called themselves *Nundawaono,* "People of the Great Hill."
Sequoia (Seh-kwōy´-yah). [Cherokee] name of the man who codified the

Cherokee language into a syllabic script in the early 18th century.

shaman (shah´-mun). An Asian term referring to one who speaks with ancestral spirits in order to heal or gain power. Often applied by Europeans to Native American medicine men.

Siksika (Sēēk-sēē´-ka). *See* Blackfoot. name of a northern plains—northwest people, "Black Moccasins."

Sioux (Sū). *See* Dakota. corruption of an Anishinabe word meaning "Snakes," which refers to those who call themselves *Dakota* or *Lakota* or *Nakota* or *Ocheti shakowin*—the "Seven Council Fires."

sipapu (See-pah´-pu). [Hopi] the hole through which the people emerged into this world from the one below it. Every kiva has a sipapu in its floor.

Spirit Dogs. Name which some of the Plains Indians gave to the horse when it appeared in the 17th or 18th century. Their largest domestic animal prior to the horse had been the dog.

Sumig (Suh´-mig). [Yurok] place name on California coast.

Tabaldak (Ta-bal-dak´). [Abenaki] name for the Creator; means the "Owner."

Tehanetorens (Dey´-ha-ne-dō-lens). [Mohawk (Iroquois)] name of Ray Fadden, an Iroquois Mohawk teacher; means "He is looking through the pine trees."

tipi (tēē´-pēē). [Siouan] Plains Indian dwelling, a cone-shaped house of skins over a frame of poles; means "dwelling."

Tlingit (Klin´-kit). A native people of the Pacific Northwest.

totem (tō´-tum). [Anishinabe] refers to the animal relatives regarded as ancestral to the lineage. Each person is born into a particular totem, inherited in many native cultures through the mother. Totem animals include Bear, Eagle, Deer, Turtle, Wolf, Snipe, Eel and many others. Common throughout North America.

tribe. From Latin *tribus*. a term used by both Indians and non-Indians to refer to groups of Native Americans sharing common linguistic and cultural heritage. Some Native American people prefer to speak not of "tribe" but of nation.

Tsimshian (Shim´-she-un).A native people of the Pacific Northwest.

Tunka-shila (Toon-kah´-shē-lah). [Lakota (Siouan)] refers to the Creator or one of the Great Benevolent Forces of nature, "Grandfather Rock."

Tuscarora (Tus-ka-rō´-rah).The sixth nation of the Iroquois who were driven by the Europeans from the lands in North Carolina in the early 18th century and resettled in western New York State; means "Shirt-wearers."

Wabanaki Confederacy (Wa´-bah-na-kēē). A loose union of a number of Abenaki nations circa 1750-1850 possibly echoing an earlier confederacy and influenced by the Iroquois League. Allied Micmac, Maliseet, Passamaquoddy, Penobscot and Abenaki. Wampum belts were introduced and triannual meetings held at Caughnawaga, Quebec.

Wakan Tanka (Wah-kon´ Tōn´-kah). [Lakota (Siouan)] The Creator, the "Great Mystery."

Wampanoag (wom-pah-nō´-ag). Means "Dawn People," sometimes called

Pokanoket. Algonquian linguistic group of eastern woodlands which once occupied what are now Bristol County, Rhode Island, and Bristol County, Massachusetts. Many were killed, along with the Narragansetts, by the colonists in "King Philip's War" in 1675 (King Philip was the colonists' name for Chief Metacomet, son of Massasoit). At least 500 Wampanoag live today on Martha's Vineyard, Nantucket and other places in the region.

wigwam (wig´-wom). [Abenaki] probably from *wetuom*, which means "dwelling." Dome-shaped house made from bent sticks covered with bark, common to northeastern Abenaki peoples.

Wuchowsen (Wōō-kow´-sun). [Abenaki] the wind bird.

Yahi. *See* Yana.

Yana or **Yahi** (Yah´-nah or Yah´-hēē). A native people of California.

Yokuts (yō´-kuts). Means "person." Among the most numerous of the California—West Coast Indian groups. Probably once numbered 10,000, including a population in the San Joaquin Valley; today they number less than 600.

Yurok (Yū´-rok). A native people of northern California.

Zuni (Zōō´-ñēē). [ñ = nasalized] A Pueblo people of New Mexico who call themselves *Ashiwi*, the "Flesh." Name comes from a Keresan Pueblo word whose meaning is unknown.

Tribal Nation Descriptions

Abenaki(Ab'-eh-na-kee). The Abenaki, or "People of the Dawn Land," are found in eastern North America along the U.S.–Canadian border. Today there are sizable Abenaki settlements near Swanton, Vermont, and at the Odanak Reserve on the St. Francis River in Quebec. Smaller Abenaki communities exist throughout Vermont and New Hampshire and parts of southern Quebec. Their language is part of the Algonquian family, and before the coming of the Europeans, they lived in small villages and changed locations seasonally, depending on such factors as the salmon runs, the ripening of berries or the arrival of deer-hunting season. Their pre-Columbian residences were called *wigwams,* small birch-covered houses which were either cone- or dome-shaped or sometimes shaped like a longhouse. Many of their stories are about Gluscabi, "One Who Tells Stories," a character who lived before the humans came and who sometimes made mistakes with his great powers and other times helped his "Children's Children," the Abenaki. Abenaki men and women were well known to their white neighbors from the sixteenth through the early twentieth centuries as traditional healers, midwives, guides and snowshoe and basket makers.

Anishinabe (Ah-nish-ih-nah'-bey). The Anishinabe, or the "People," are also known as the Chippewa (in the United States) or the Ojibway (in Canada), names that may refer to the puckered style of moccasins they wore. A people of the Great Lakes region, they also spoke an Algonquian language, and they developed a pictograph style of writing on birch bark that was used to tell some of their most sacred stories. One of the heroes of their tales was Manabozho, who is the character Longfellow was actually writing about in his "Song of Hiawatha" (Hiawatha was an Iroquois political leader). Their way of life included agriculture, fishing, hunting and rice gathering from the headwaters of the Mississippi. Today the Anishinabe are one of the most numerous of the native nations, with about 160,000 people living in Michigan, Wisconsin,

Minnesota, North Dakota and southern Ontario. Some live on reservations, such as Turtle Mountain, White Earth and Leech Lake, but there are also large communities of Anishinabe people in such cities as Minneapolis and St. Paul.

Blackfeet. The Blackfeet (Blackfoot in Canada) call themselves *Siksika* (sik-sih'-ka), meaning "Those with the Black-dyed Moccasins." Their traditional lands encompassed the northwest plains and mountains, and Blackfeet communities exist today in northern Montana and southern Alberta. Hunters of the buffalo, they lived in cone-shaped lodges covered with buffalo skin; they would symbolize yearly events or even legends by drawing pictures on buffalo skins. A wonderful collection of traditional Blackfeet stories is *The Sun Came Down* (Harper and Row, 1985), by the late Percy Bullchild. Jim Welch, one of the finest contemporary Native American writers, published a powerful historical novel about his Blackfeet ancestors, *Fools Crow* (Viking Penguin, 1988).

Cherokee (Chair-oh-key'). The Cherokee called themselves the *Ani-yunwiya*, meaning "Real Human Beings," but the name they are known by is a corruption of the Choctaw word *Chillaiki*, or "People of the Cave Country." Their language is of the Iroquoian family, and their traditional lands included most of North Carolina, South Carolina, and Georgia. They lived in large villages with extensive gardens, but they so quickly adopted European ways, clothing and residences, while still maintaining their own customs and languages, that they were called (along with the Seminole, Creek, Chickasaw and Choctaw) the "Five Civilized Tribes." After gold was discovered on their lands in the early 1800s, they were forced to relocate to the Indian Territory (later called Oklahoma) along the "Trail of Tears." Ten thousand Cherokee died along that trail. Some, however, sought refuge in the North Carolina mountains, and today two Cherokee national communities exist, one in Oklahoma and one in North Carolina. Perhaps the most famous Cherokee was a scholar named Sequoia, who codified a syllabic alphabet for the Cherokee in the early eighteenth century. Within twenty years of its development, virtually all of the Cherokee people could read and write using this alphabet, and newspapers were published in the syllabary.

Creek (Kreek). The Creek people are one of the "Five Civilized Tribes" who were forced to leave their lands in the southeast and migrate to the Indian Territory between 1836 and 1840. They were named "Creek" by the English, who observed that their villages were always near small streams. They called themselves Muskogee, and their language is similar to that of the Choctaw and the Seminole, who are actually an offshoot of the Lower Creek Nation. Their original homelands stretched along the

Atlantic Coast from Georgia through Alabama. They brought many of their traditional village names and family structures with them to Oklahoma, as well as traditional religious practices, songs and Stomp Dances, which are carefully maintained to this day. One of their most important ball games was a forerunner of contemporary hockey. Corn was an important staple for the Creeks, and to this day the Green Corn Ceremonial is the peak of their annual religious celebrations. Today the highly progressive Creek Nation is organized into nineteen towns in eastern Oklahoma, with its central offices in Okmulgee.

Dakota. *See* Sioux.

Hopi (Ho'-pee). The name is a contraction of *Hopitu,* the "Peaceful Ones," and the Hopi are, indeed, a people of peace who have a long history of resolving conflicts through means other than warfare. Their extremely sophisticated knowledge of dry-land farming has enabled them to survive in the arid mesa regions of what is now northern Arizona, where their multilevel, multiple-residency structures of adobe and wood have stood for centuries. Some Hopi buildings have been continuously inhabited for more than five hundred years. The Hopi's artistic traditions include weaving and pottery, both of which they say were given them by the benevolent Grandmother Spider, who is seen as one of the primary creative forces. Hopi prophecies speak of past worlds destroyed by misdeeds and of a possibile future cataclysm if human beings do not follow a way of life in balance with the natural world and all its beings. Their present-day lands are completely surrounded by the huge Navajo reservation.

Iroquois (Ear'-oh-kwah). The word *Iroquois* is a corruption of the Abenaki word *Ireokwa,* which means "Real Snakes." Their language is related to that of the Sioux and the Cherokee, and their traditions tell of a migration from the west.The Iroquois people were originally five nations—the Mohawk, the Oneida, the Onondaga, the Cayuga and the Seneca. Their traditional territory included most of present-day New York State, from the Hudson River to the Niagara. Centuries ago, the five nations were engaged in constant warfare until a man known as the Peacemaker was sent to them by the Creator. With the aid of Hiawatha and the woman known as Jigonsaseh, the Peacemaker formed a league of peace, unity and strength symbolized by a great white pine tree with a vigilant eagle perched atop it clutching five arrows. This Iroquois League was apparently an important influence on the formation of the U.S. system of government and on the drafting of the U.S. Constitution. The Iroquois lived in large bark longhouses, each house holding as many as sixty people and headed by a clan mother. At its height, the Iroquois

League controlled an area of the northeast larger than the old Roman Empire, and the Iroquois's alliance with the British tipped the balance against the French in controlling the continent. The Iroquois have always prided themselves on diplomacy, and to this day, Iroquois traditional leaders travel the world speaking of peace. Iroquois people today are found on thirteen reservations and reserves in New York State, Quebec, Ontario and Wisconsin.

Kalispel (Kahl-ih-spell'). Neighbors of the Nez Percé, the Colvilles and the Flatheads, the Kalispel are a native people of the northwest, in what is today the states of Washington and Idaho. Their language belongs to the Salish language family. Like their neighbors, the Kalispel built fish racks and spearing platforms and fished the abundant runs of salmon that came up the rivers. They also used many of the roots and bulbs growing in the area, especially the camas root. In fact, their name appears to refer to the camas. They are also known as the *Pend d'Oreille,* or "Ear Drops," a reference to the pendant earrings they wore. The present-day reservation is located near Usk, north of Spokane, Washington.

Lakota. *See* Sioux.

Micmac (Mihk'-mahk). The name means "Our Allies" in Abenaki. One of the Wabanaki nations, the Micmac people lived, as they do today, primarily in the maritime provinces of Canada—Nova Scotia, New Brunswick and Prince Edward Island. Their way of life was balanced between land and sea, and like their Abenaki cousins, they migrated seasonally to various hunting and fishing grounds. Hunting, fishing and virtually everything in their universe, including mountains and rivers, is seen as alive, and respect for the animals, birds and fish is an important factor in their way of life, their stories and their traditional practices. One of the most important native nations of the northeast, the Micmac number more than fifteen thousand people today in Canada and the United States.

Muskogee. *See* Creek.

Navajo (Nav'-uh-ho). The Navajo call themselves *Dine,* which means the "People." They are the most numerous of the native nations in the United States with over 200,000 people, most of whom live on the huge Navajo Reservation. Covering 15 million acres in the Four Corners area where the states of New Mexico, Arizona, Colorado and Utah come together, the Navajo Reservation is the size of West Virginia. The reservation itself is spectacularly beautiful, although much of it is arid. At present, the lands of the Navajo and their traditional ways of life are being seriously threatened by commercial mining interests that wish to strip much of the land for coal and uranium.

The Navajo, like the Apache (who called themselves *Tineh*), are close relatives of the Athabascan peoples of Alaska and the northwest and speak a similar language. They migrated from the north to the southwest more than one thousand years ago. The name *Navajo*, which means "Enemy People," was given to them by the original residents of the southwest, the Pueblo peoples, whose villages they often raided. The typical Navajo dwelling is an eight-sided, dome-shaped, single-family structure called a *hogan*.

The Navajo believe that balance is the natural human state and that sickness is caused by imbalance. The word *hozho*, which appears in Navajo healing chants such as the Beautyway, means both balance and beauty. Their stories, which are similar to those of their Pueblo neighbors, are incorporated into their healing ceremonies as sand paintings picturing characters from traditional tales. Since the 1800s, the formerly nomadic Navajo have been herders of sheep, and they are widely known for their beautifully woven wool blankets.

Nisqually (Nis-kwah'-lee). Another of the "salmon culture" people of the Pacific Northwest, the Nisqually originally settled around the Salish River, which empties into Puget Sound. They are members of the Salish language family. Their current reservation is on the Nisqually River, near Olympia, Washington. Like other native people of the area, they have strong traditions about the volcanic mountains of their homeland, seeing them as living beings with individual personalities. Native friends from that area who said that *Loo-Wit* was not happy with the way people were treating her predicted the mid-1970s eruption of Mount Saint Helen.

Onondaga. *See* Iroquois.

Pawnee (Paw'-nee). *Pawnee* means "horn." It refers to the traditional hairstyle of the men, who shaved the hair from the sides of their heads and then stiffened the hair on top with buffalo grease so that it resembled a horn. The Pawnee called themselves *Chahiksichahiks*, which means "Men of Men." Their traditional dwellings were large dome-shaped earth lodges, and their original territory included the same high plains area where the Sioux and the Cheyenne lived. The Pawnee had a reputation as farmers and peaceful people, although they were also skillful hunters of the buffalo. Today there are four bands of Pawnee living in and around the town of Pawnee in Southern Oklahoma.

Seneca. *See* Iroquois.

Sioux (Su). Sioux is the corruption of an Algonquian word meaning "Snakes." Those people of the plains called themselves *Dakota* (Eastern Sioux) or *Lakota* (Western Sioux). They also called themselves *Ocheti Lakowin*, "The Seven Council Fires." They are, in the popular imagination, perhaps the best known of the native nations of North America. Their tipis, feathered head-dresses, buffalo-hunting way of life and horse culture (which was developed entirely after the 1500s) have become the very image of what "Indians" should look like. There is no doubt that their traditional way of life, which stressed generosity, honor, personal courage, fortitude, cooperation and a careful use of the natural world around them, was attractive and admirable. Their stories reflect these qualities. Sadly, the continuing history of relations between the U.S. government and the various Sioux nations also reflects how little the U.S. has understood or respected these proud and highly principled people. Great Americans such as Crazy Horse, Red Cloud, and Sitting Bull are among the Sioux leaders whose names are familiar all around the world. Traditional Sioux territory stretched from Minnesota through North and South Dakota, Nebraska and Montana. There are large Sioux communities and reservations in those states today.

Tsimshian (Shim'-she-an). The Tsimshian are a people of the Pacific Northwest and their culture was similar to that of their neighbors, the Haida, the Tlingit, the Kwakiutl, Chinook and others. These native peoples relied upon and showed great respect for the ocean, which produced their main food source, salmon. It was their belief that the salmon came from the ocean to feed the people and so their ceremonies had to express the proper gratitude to the salmon. They were great carvers of wood, making large wooden houses, sea-going canoes and huge and intricate totem poles (which depicted important animals and spirits, incidents and beings from their stories, such as Raven). The Tsimshian were especially well known as traders who went up and down the northwest coast trading copper, dentalium shells and otter skins. Today there is a small community of Tsimshian people in southeast Alaska, but the bulk of the population lives further south along the Canadian coast.

Yurok (Yu'-rock). Yurok, a word from the nearby Karok Indian people's language, means a "Distance down the River" or the "People Downriver." They call themselves *Olekw'ol*, which means "Persons." Their language is of the Algic language family, distantly related to the Algonquian tongues of the east. The traditional lands of the Yurok people are along the mouth of the Klamath river in what is now northern California. Since food was abundant, making it possible for them to live in settled villages without the need for seasonal migration, they built permanent houses from wooden planks. Shellfish, deer, salmon, acorns, elk and sea lions were among their important foods. Though never numbering more than a few thousand people, they possessed an extremely rich ceremonial life. Their language is highly complex, reflecting their social structure, which once included what could only be described as an aristocratic class, whose speech was quite different from that of the common people. Today the Yurok people still live in the region of the lower Klamath River, near Trinidad and Klamath, California.

Zuni (Zoo'-nee). The Zuni call themselves *Siwi,* a name whose meaning is not known. Their traditional homeland is along the banks of the Zuni River, in the two-hundred-square-mile area just west of the Continental Divide on the border between New Mexico and Arizona. They were among the first of the Pueblo peoples to be visited by Europeans when the Spanish under Coronado attacked them in 1540. The Spanish believed that the city of Hawikuh was one of the fabled "Seven Cities of Cibola," filled with gold and silver like the cities of the Aztecs. Such cities never existed, but the Spanish called the region "Cibola" for years after. The Zuni's present-day population of about six thousand people makes them the largest of the Pueblo nations. The Zuni are a highly philosophical and religious people, and many of their ceremonies remain closed to all outsiders. However, the great early winter celebration of Shalako, one of the most spectacular of all native ceremonies, remains open to all who come. The poetic nature of their songs and stories is shown in recent translations of Zuni narratives, such as Dennis Tedlock's *Finding the Center* (Dial, 1972).

Keepers of the Earth

An extraordinary teaching tool to introduce children to the natural world

By Michael J. Caduto and Joseph Bruchac

✣ **Keepers of the Earth: Native Stories and Environmental Activities for Children** is a wonderful resource for teachers, naturalists, parents and outdoor educators. Each story is followed by questions and activities that foster an appreciation for the natural world. For children ages 5–12.
ISBN: 0-920079-57-1, $22.95

✣ **Teacher's Guide for Keepers of the Earth** includes teaching ideas, resources for environmental studies, storytelling and values education. An extensive bibliography for adults and children is provided for each chapter of *Keepers of the Earth*. ISBN: 1-55591-040-8, $9.95

✣ **Keepers of the Earth Audiocassette Tape** is a two-tape set representing the complete, unabridged stories from *Keepers of the Earth,* told by the well-known Abenaki storyteller, Joseph Bruchac.
ISBN: 0-920079-86-5, $16.95

Coming Fall 1991
✣ **Keepers of the Animals: Native Stories and Wildlife Activities for Children** continues the tradition established by *Keepers of the Earth*. This new collection of Native stories holds power and wisdom to help us learn to live in balance with other life on earth. Focusing on the importance of animals in Native storytelling, this book offers questions and activities that foster an appreciation for all living things. For children ages 5–12.
ISBN: 0-920079-88-1, price to be announced

Fifth House Publishers
620 Duchess Street
Saskatoon, SK
S7K 0R1